Also by Hope Sheffield

Blood Mother

The Inflatable Man

Hope Sheffield

Turnabout

This is a work of fiction. Names and characters are a product of the
author's imagination, and any resemblance to actual persons, living
or dead, is entirely coincidental.

To my husband Jeff,

with love and gratitude

Chapter One

Michael Fisher reached across the bed toward his wife, Nicole, with what he hoped was romantic fervor. Ever since she cheated on him sixteen months ago, on October 13, 1995, on a business trip in Disneyworld, Michael had made a solid effort to become whatever she obviously was missing in bed. Honestly, he wasn't quite sure what to do.

At first he thought maybe quantity was the problem. Since they were both hardworking lawyers at Winters & Early in downtown Chicago, they naturally put in long days at the firm, plus frequent calls to their answering machines to handle legal questions that arose after they finally arrived home. Their twin teenage daughters, Abby and Kelsey, needed chauffeuring to and from parties and school activities, and there just wasn't a lot of time left, what with commuting and sleeping. Sixteen months ago, when he pecked Nicole goodbye before she zipped off to a litigation celebration in Orlando after six monastic days, it never occurred to

Michael that this small sex-free period might create in her some unconquerable need to pick up a man in a bar and wrestle him to the nearest bed. Honestly, Michael barely thought of Nicole as a sexual being, despite the fact that they engaged in that activity most Saturday nights. She always seemed willing, but frankly uninspired. He had assumed she was happy with the once-a-week situation. He had even felt pretty proud of their sex lives -- he thought a lot of lawyers probably did it a lot less, under the circumstances.

But maybe the problem was quality. Tentatively, Michael stroked Nicole's shoulder, his fingers nudging under the strap of her red negligee. She seemed to be considering closing her book. When she kept reading, he was never sure if it was because she wasn't interested or because she just liked to be seduced. Well, he was going with the seduced theory these days, based on her past performance, or at least as much of it as he could stand to get out of her. He leaned behind the book – ow, a corner, damn it! – and smooched gently but damply at her cheek.

"Really, Michael?" she said, her mouth pinched in a schoolmarmy way, but she set the book down on the bedside table and turned toward him cooperatively.

So, what would Jesus do, he pondered – well, not Jesus of course, more like Alejandro or maybe Ian, the suave foreign lover who had persuaded his 45-year-old lawyer wife of twenty years into his hotel room at Disney's Polynesian Resort on a steamy Florida night a year ago last October. Michael placed his hands on her hips as he shifted on top of her and forcefully kissed her neck. He heard Nicole make a choking sound but decided to ignore it.

"Honey, please," she coughed, and it exploded his heart like a bullet murdering him for the millionth time, how much she had risked to allow this strange man to lie on top of her – their marriage, the girls, her health, possibly even her own life – just to have twenty minutes naked with Alejandro the drunken salesman.

"Sorry."

He decided to kiss her mouth instead, although Nicole had assured him that Alejandro had not done that, it was too personal. That had been a comfort – odd, considering what they had done, but Nicole made their actual union sound clumsy, unpleasant, and strangely remote -- as remote as two naked people touching at various private points could possibly be. On a good day, on the train to work or shoveling snow or in the shower, Michael was able to imagine them touching only at the vital place, eyes averted, hands primly at their sides or flailing ineffectually in the air. But whenever he and Nicole were having sex -- which was frequent these days, he was not giving Nicole's libido any opportunity to resurface -- Michael always imagined Alejandro's technique in nauseating detail and compared it unfavorably to his own. Of course Nicole had told him as little as possible – she claimed drunken amnesia for details – but he could feel every steamy slurp and writhe as the twist of his intestines during disembowelment.

Nicole started kicking. "It's so hot, with all these blankets. Just a sec." She gave him a gentle push and sat up, whipping her nightie over her head. "There, that's better," and she reclined back down beside him and leaned up for a kiss.

Alejandro must have seen her like this. She was so lovely, in spite of her forty-five years and the work and the stress and the kids. She was more beautiful than when he had married her -- somehow the thin laugh lines framing her soft brown eyes and the angularity of her aging cheekbones suited her. Conforming to professional expectations, she wore her hair straight, but the steam from her pre-bed shower had released a few endearing dark curls, softening her features. Looking at her now, he could still see the girl she was when he met her in law school, a ghost shimmering behind the creases and the softening jaw line. He knew that, despite his sickening physical intimacy – Nicole, how could you, how could you? – Alejandro couldn't see that ghost. No one else had known her so long or loved her like he did. The only thing that made her indiscretion slightly tolerable – because it had become a horrible part of him, he had thought about it every single day for the last sixteen months and feared that this was just his life now, he would always think about it, especially when they made love, which was practically constant – the only thing that allowed him to continue on as a basically stable human being, was that Nicole's lover had been a complete stranger, a drunken fling, whose name she

4

didn't even know, and whom she would never, ever see again.

Nicole kissed Michael's cheek and reached up to stroke his thinning dark hair. Then she leaned back against the pillow and closed her eyes. She would never have touched him so gently, so lovingly, before, she thought, sixteen months ago, two thousand years ago, when sex was the stiff and mechanical symbol of a decade of routine and resentment. Sixteen months ago, when she could barely look at Michael, their lives had appeared to be perfect. After years of saving from almost constant work as partners at Winters & Early, they took a leap and a jumbo mortgage to buy a riparian house on Lake Michigan in east Wilmette. The house itself wasn't much, an old brick cottage barely big enough for their family of four, and it needed work, according to local standards. The kitchen had no island, the washer and dryer were in the basement, and the bathrooms – well, you had to shower standing in the tub even in the master bath, which was a lot to ask from owners of a $2 million North Shore house. But the backyard was amazing, long and narrow with several bio zones: first, a landscaped patio with sculpted boxwoods and overstuffed urns spilling nasturtiums onto the flagstone; next, sandy hills with dune grasses and a few discreet, sloping wooden chairs, where she could sip her coffee and catch up on paperwork on warm mornings; and finally, the beach, their own slice of soft, brown sand gradually disappearing into the smooth, ice blue lake on calm mornings, or roiling, white waves after a storm. The lake changed daily, but somehow provided a sense of permanence and serenity which centered and lifted her. Nicole knew, when she felt the lake breeze, and when the water cooled her feet as she watched the curved horizon, that her life was good, that despite any rough spots in her marriage or in her relationship with her daughters, the bedrock was good, and things would come around. All relationships had their rough patches, the trick was not to give up, to ride them out, even if those patches lasted for years.

All that was gone now. She had destroyed it. Nicole peered over Michael's shoulder at the bedroom window facing their new backyard, barely big enough to hold a small cement patio and an old stucco garage opening onto the alley. Sixteen months ago, shaken by her indiscretion, Nicole returned from Florida seeking forgiveness. She needed to confess, she needed to be cleansed, and she had not realized that this need of hers would be so painful for her husband. Michael was a lawyer, she thought he would understand the distinction -- this wasn't an affair, it was just one night, one horrible mistake, she hadn't even enjoyed it. But Michael was shattered beyond all her imaginings. He insisted that she quit the law firm. Her job had polluted her, it had warped her values, and at the very least it created the

6

opportunity for her transgression. And he was right, he didn't even know how right he was, he could never know. Her leaving the partnership was Michael's condition for any attempt to salvage their marriage. So she quit of course, she loved him.

Then they could no longer afford the house on the lake. Well, it was only fair that she should suffer, that she should give up the beautiful view and the heavenly breeze and the position she had earned as a successful litigation partner at Winters & Early. She was the guilty one, and she loved Michael. She couldn't lose him and hurt the girls. That would be losing everything.

Nicole felt Michael shift, his chest close against her breast again as he held her, and she focused on their synchrony, each of them in the moment, feeling the other's skin, so close that they had found their other half. And she was happy now in his arms, and so relieved, knowing that they were in communion, that Michael had finally gotten over her mistake. They had put the past behind them and started fresh. They loved each other, that was the important thing. That night had been a horrible, awful mistake, and she had paid the price for it. Now they had a new life and a new appreciation for each other. That was the one good thing that came out of the whole sordid mess, and it was a very good thing. It had renewed their love. Nicole looked at Michael, his eyes closed in concentration. And then his eyes opened, and she touched his rough cheek and smiled at him. Yes, they were together, and he had forgiven her. He had finally forgotten the whole thing.

"I don't know what they do up there every night, it's kind of weird."

Lounging in an armchair in the basement rec room, Kelsey Fisher scrunched her nose at her twin sister Abby and tilted her eyes skyward. Her slim back curving over her foot, she scrutinized her toes, which she had just painted passion pink. Kelsey would so much have preferred a professional pedicure, her do-it-yourself job was ghetto. But she was low on funds just for basics since her mother had totally unfairly slashed her allowance due to recent austerity measures, the result of circumstances that were not her fault in any way, what was up with that?

Abby turned away from the credits to *Sex and the City* scrolling perkily on the television screen. "I don't know," she responded, "I've thought about it. Do you think they're still talking about Mom's – thing?"

They both knew about Mom's, well, mistake. Nobody had told them, but they had ears, right? And they were seniors in high school, they weren't exactly babies. But it was so messed up. Men did stuff like that. That's why Hooters and bachelor parties got invented. Moms were supposed to have headaches.

"Beats me. If they are it's like, ridiculous. That happened eons ago, and it was totally gross, but they need to get over themselves. Whatever it is, I'm not going near their bedroom until they come out of it, that's all I'm saying." Kelsey looked meaningfully at Abby and winced.

"I don't get what you're worried about. I mean, I don't hear them yelling or anything." Abby pulled her brown cardigan tightly to her chest. "Jeez, it's cold down here. I miss the old house."

"Abby, you're such a loser."

Kelsey fluffed her blonde curls and studied her sister. Yes, they were twins, but completely fraternal, they looked absolutely nothing alike. Besides Kelsey's natural prettiness, her clear skin and wide blue eyes and petite figure, she actually made something of herself. Well, she streaked her hair for starters -- just a sun-kissed look, all the New Trier girls did it, thank god Mom hadn't eliminated that crucial expense. And so what if she had to lie down to zip her jeans, her butt looked totally tight, and her skimpy tank tops showed her belly button ring and the tiniest glimpse of cleavage to good advantage. Yes, it was February, yes, she did suffer in flu season, but there was no way she was wearing a ratty old maid cardigan like Abby, who took no interest at all in trying to look her best. Sure, Abby had to wait in the snow for the bus to come take her to school, while Kelsey got a cozy ride with her boyfriend Brandon in his

9

Audi TT -- but that was a chicken-egg problem, wasn't it?

"Which reminds me," Kelsey continued. "I ran into Mrs. Bennett this morning. She was wondering if either of us could babysit for a couple hours tomorrow night. Those kids are big, it's a pretty sweet deal, but I'm having dinner with Brandon then, so I told her I'd ask you."

"Sure, I guess I could." Abby got up off the faded gray rug, swept her brown hair into a terry cloth scrunchy, and started running in place. "Yeah, I have an A.P. physics test on Thursday, but I like Maggie and Lucy, and they aren't much trouble. I don't even think they need a babysitter. It must be because their mom does stuff with criminals. She's probably seen too much. I am so cold! I wonder if she could arrest Mr. Bigelow for buying our house under false pretenses and then messing up the beach. That has to be a crime against humanity or something."

"Yeah. You should ask her." Even Kelsey, who was hardly some veggie eco weirdo, was upset about the old homestead. The timeline went something like this:

1. Mom has gross-out, drunken middle-aged cheating sex with some unknown dude from a tiki bar at the Polynesian Resort in Disneyworld and comes home and, brilliant, tells Dad about it.

2. Dad goes completely ballistic, duh, and makes Mom quit her super well-paid job as a

10

way important partner at Winters & Early, even though the job has, like, nothing to do with it, and Mom is really, really sorry.

3. Now they are destitute and have to barely survive on Dad's meager salary as a much less important partner, meaning no more pedicures, and that they have to move.

4. Mr. Winston Bigelow, a super rich old guy partner at the same Chicago law firm, swoops in to buy their fun and classy house on the lake with cash money and many professions of love and adoration for the house, the yard, the view, and the beach.

5. The impoverished Fisher family moves into an embarrassing old stucco house literally on the other side of the tracks in squalid west Wilmette.

6. Mr. Creepy Backstabber Liar Winston Bigelow immediately tears down their old house and builds a deluxe McMansion which sprawls all over the place and then, the cherry on the cupcake of their delight, begins construction on a huge and heinous beach house six inches from the water and practically sloshing over into their neighbors' yards. Which environmentally unfriendly and property-value-reducing eyesore has been splattered all over the *Wilmette Life*, because the neighbors are pissed off and suing right

and left, and Mom and Dad are totally destroyed too. They loved that old place, and now it is kaput.

"I can't believe that Bigelow guy," said Kelsey. "Somebody ought to, I don't know, drown him in the lake."

"Cool. Poetic justice," Abby noted uncertainly.

"Which also reminds me," Kelsey continued, arching her back so that her belly button jewel glinted in the light from the bare bulb overhead, "in a bizarre twist of fate, we are actually all meeting for pictures at the Bigelows' on Saturday night before Turnabout. So tell Freddy."

"That is weird. Anyway, I don't know if I still want to go, Kels. It's not really my scene."

"I don't even want to think about your scene, Abby, you're going to this dance. You asked Freddy, he actually accepted -- this is your moment to quit mooning over him and finally go out. We're seniors, this is it, last chance before toll road. You want to see what a New Trier dance is like, don't you? I wouldn't go except for you, I am totally over it, but this is something you have to do, or You'll Regret It for the Rest of Your Life. I mean, no offense, but it's not like the guy is going to ask you to Prom."

Abby stopped running. "Not nice, but okay. You're still coming shopping Thursday with me and Mom, right?"

"Course. You're my sister, and I want you to look foxy." Yeah, right, Kelsey was totally going for passable. Everybody knew that Abby and Kelsey were sisters, and if Abby looked bizarre, that might reflect poorly on Kelsey's own coolness. Besides, she really did want Abby to have fun. After all that Social Service Board and Academic Bowl, the girl really needed an unforgettable night.

Kelsey stood up and took Abby's arm. "Come on, let's go upstairs, I'll make us some hot tea. It's probably safe by now."

Chapter Two

Clattering down the brick street toward home, Pamela Bigelow looked out the windows of her Lexus in awe. To her right, the trunks and branches of the old oaks and chestnut trees in Gillson Park stood white with a rim of new snow against the gray winter sky. Across the expanse of lawn, icy and bleak, past the empty tennis courts and the frozen playground, she glimpsed the lake, like a frosty drink sloshing in an enormous bowl. To her left were large houses, brick and stone, and then the country club, for those who preferred their water in swimming pools and Perrier bottles. As she continued, the houses on the right became more majestic, their backyard sandy beaches in a continuous flow from the public beach, separated only by a sign reading, "Private Property."

In front of her own cobblestone driveway, Pam put on the blinker, right turn, but there was no need. No other cars were driving here, on the most exclusive street in Wilmette. The only people outside on this cold afternoon were a couple of workers unraveling Christmas lights from the hedge across the street. Pam remembered her childhood, her father spending all day winding strings of large colored bulbs around the evergreens in their modest front yard, and her excitement and his pride when he illuminated them each night. Here, homeowners could afford to hire professionals to construct elaborate displays with hundreds of lights, thousands probably, artistically outlining their tallest trees with tiny white bulbs. Despite fifteen years as the wife of Winston Bigelow, the head of litigation at the law firm Winters & Early, despite years of elegant dinners and Turks and Caicos vacations and shoes from Neiman-Marcus, Pam still could not quite believe that she lived here, in a brand new lakefront home on this fancy street.

Pulling into the circular drive, she parked in front of the double front doors and stared up at the house. It was three stories from walkout basement to roof, a mud colored stucco that filled the lot from side to side and then projected deep into the back, and designed to resemble a Tuscan villa that Winston had seen in *Architectural Digest*. She remembered the house that used to sit here, a snug brick cottage that sank inconspicuously into the lot and made the entire property appear to be just the garage of the grand stone house to its north. Frankly, she would have been happy to live in the cottage. It had all the space a family of three needed, and it wasn't in bad shape. But Winston had a vision. When no one had believed that an Italianate mansion could be built on such a narrow lot, he and the architects put their considerable intelligence together and used every inch that the Village allowed. Really, she supposed that Winston was right. The villa was quite beautiful, and the earlier house did not reflect the grandeur of the street.

Of course the neighbors would have preferred that they tear down the cottage and leave the land vacant. Well, they could have bought the old house and done that themselves, if they were such green space advocates. And now they were making an enormous fuss over the new beach house, when they all had beach houses themselves. To be honest, Pam hadn't been sure they needed a beach house. But Winston pointed out that it wasn't a question of need in a case like this. Ricky and his friends might enjoy it, and anyway they had a right to it, even if it were bigger and closer to the water than all the other ones. What was the point of a beach house if it were up next to the main house?

Bracing herself, Pam opened the car door and stepped her sneakered foot daintily into the slush. Teaching yoga did not require the same degree of exertion as taking the class, and her spandex shorts were not sufficient coverage for February in Chicago. She picked her way to the front doors, fumbled in her purse for the key, and opened the one on the right. Finally, after a year of building and the last couple of months of tinkering with final touches, the workmen were gone, and Pam could enjoy a light lunch alone in her fabulous

16

kitchen with its granite island, double ovens, and stylish hanging pot rack. Pulling off her damp shoes, she anticipated a little of the tuna salad she had picked up at the Italian deli a few blocks away, and maybe a few of those convenient prepared carrot sticks from the Jewel. That and a big mug of hot tea brewed in the microwave, and she would recover fully from her teaching session. Brrr, it was cold even in the house, with its twelve foot ceilings and big windows onto the lake and Winston's insistence that they emulate the Europeans, who apparently keep the heat low and wear piles of bulky sweaters. Well, maybe, since he was at work, she would sneak the heat up just a tad.

"Hello, Pam."

As she reached for the living room thermostat, Winston popped his silvery head out from behind a miniature olive tree.

Pam jumped back in surprise. "You're home early. Did you forget something?"

"Not at all. I want to talk to you."

Pam was ravenous and looking forward to the meager meal that she allowed herself so that she could look the way Winston liked, so that he would be proud to introduce her as his wife at partner dinners and charitable events. But in the fifteen years that they had been married, she could not remember a single time that Winston had appeared at home on a weekday before 7:00 p.m. Even when she had gone into labor with Ricky early one Thursday morning, he had insisted that he must go to work, and that she must delay producing the baby until that night if she wanted him to attend. Well, as he had pointed out, that was why they had so many nice things, because he worked hard to support their lifestyle. And she had listened. She always listened to Winston, he was usually right. And now he wanted to talk with her, in person, at 12:30 on a Wednesday? Pam felt her stomach flip from hungry to ill. That was a new one, and it couldn't be good.

Standing gravely, Winston pushed back his shoulders, extending his body to its full six feet, and calmly studied Pam. He had worked hard to create the right environment in this house, a serene old world Italian feel, with the lake representing the Mediterranean, only at this time of year a lot colder. And there Pam stood, her frosted hair swept into a juvenile ponytail, her small chest further flattened by the spandex sports bra that she insisted on wearing to the yoga class she taught in a pitiable attempt to fill her empty days. Here she was, forty years old, a grown woman with an important husband and an adolescent son -- and still she was just going through the motions of life, keeping busy, exercising and eating and sleeping. She could get away with it when she was younger, when he first met her. Then he enjoyed looking at her and touching her and the

18

envious way other men stared at him when he shepherded her around. And she had energy, a youthful vigor that lifted his spirits too. But now, look at her in that degrading outfit, and turning up the heat. She had no internal glow, that was her problem. She had no fire in her soul.

"Please, Pam, come sit next to me."

"In the living room?"

"Yes, yes, in the living room."

Winston held out his arm toward her graciously, summoning her into the formal area, the beige couch perfectly positioned on the golden oak floor facing the glass wall between them and the lake. The water looked so close, it was almost in the room with them, its icy blue lapping toward their toes.

The phone rang. Pam turned and rushed toward the kitchen, with Winston following at a leisurely pace.

"Yes, we do plan to build the beach house – well, we've already started. I'm sorry the neighbors don't like it, but, really, it isn't any of their business, is it?"

Pam was flustered, tripping over her words. She clearly had no experience with this kind of thing. Winston took the phone from her hand.

"Hello, who is this? How did you get this number? Well, I'm sure you local reporters find this sort of trivia interesting, but I don't want you bothering my wife. Suffice it to say, we are well within our rights to enhance our property as we see fit. Good day."

Winston hung up. Pam sat on a chair in the breakfast room, rested her head on the distressed Tuscan farmhouse table, and started to cry.

"There, there, Dear, no need to trouble yourself. People are idiots." He patted her on the shoulder.

"But Winston, our neighbors hate us, and now it will be in *The Wilmette Life* again, and the whole village will be talking. I'm here all the time in this house, I work at the Rec Center, I shop at the Jewel – everyone knows our business, and no one is going to like us. It's easier for you, you go downtown every day, these aren't your people. This is my home more than yours."

Winston sighed. Frankly, he was a little offended. Pam would never have come up with this house on her own, all the thought and detail that went into the design and its execution, and she certainly couldn't have paid for it with the pin money she earned teaching yoga. Without him, she would be living an insignificant life, probably with a public servant in a west Wilmette split level – maybe even in Glenview, miles from the lake -- a house that some builder had mass-produced for similar public servants back in the Fifties. That was Pam, passively taking the easy route instead of applying herself to figure out the perfect life and then make it happen. Well, that's what he needed to talk with her about.

*

Pam sheltered her head in her arms for as long as she dared. The patting had stopped, her eyes felt wet and bleary, and she needed to blow her nose. She pulled herself up to see Winston seated rigidly beside her, his eyes focused on the white waves rushing toward them and slipping away.

"What, Winston, why are you home?"

"Well, Pam, I must tell you." He paused for emphasis. "I have been thinking about my life. I am 58 years old, I am turning 59 this year, and soon I will be – no longer young. I have come to view my life as a series of episodes, each meaningful in its way, each experimenting with an aspect of human achievement, each fulfilling a personal talent or interest or aspiration of my own. Pam, we have been married, as you know, for fifteen years. I have dedicated myself to my law practice and reached its pinnacle, and I feel that it has no more to offer me. We have raised a fine son to the age of fourteen. I have provided him, and you, with material comforts, as well as the benefit of my intelligence and experience. The two of you have profited from life with me in my prime."

He paused again, significantly. Pam sat staring, her tears from the phone call forgotten smears on her sunken cheeks.

"Now I am facing a life milestone, and I cannot in good conscience ignore it. The truth is that, despite my long and excellent service, in several years I will cease to be a partner at Winters & Early. I must view this change as an opportunity to proceed to a new life episode, to take up a new challenge, to see myself in a new way. I thought that this house might be a sufficient novelty to engage me, but I realize now that I was taking the coward's path, attempting to fill my life with tasks, though creative ones, which could not provide real meaning for me. I will give you the house," he said, "but I find that I must leave it. I must move on to the next period of my life."

"You're leaving me?" Pam's eyes flooded, and she felt her head would explode. What did he mean? Was this real? They were married, they had a son and a new house and angry neighbors. What was he talking about? "Are you in love with someone else?"

Winston pushed back his chair and stood up. "I suppose that is all I could expect of you. I have thought carefully about this. It is time for me to move forward to something new, or to stay in the same patterns and die. I want to live the best life that I can, and to do that, I must probe the greatest minds in history and use them as a springboard to formulate a new life. I have decided to move to the city and enter the University of Chicago as a candidate for a PhD in philosophy. It is a noble task, I believe, and one that I must accomplish alone, unencumbered with the concerns of a suburban family."

Pam hugged her shoulders. "Don't you love me anymore?"

Winston loomed over her, his full head of silvery hair shaking with disappointment. "I'm sorry. I had somehow hoped you would understand. I have no desire to hurt you, but this is my life, and I cannot sacrifice it to protect you. That is more than one human being should ask of another. Perhaps you will come to see this as an opportunity as well. That is my wish for you."

"Are you leaving now?" She had begun to shiver uncontrollably.

"I plan to stay in the guest room until my new condominium is ready for me next week. Then I will move out. That will give you and Ricky time to adjust."

"But I don't want to live in this big house alone."

Winston turned away. "That is not my concern. That is the point." He walked to the door, opened it, and went out. In a moment, she heard the garage door hum and the rumble of his BMW. He had forgotten his coat.

Pam crumpled back onto the table top. Its solidity felt good against her face and arms. She knew Winston meant it. He was always sure of his decisions, and he never changed his mind. Maybe when I need a hug I can do this, she thought. I will lie on the table or on the floor, and I will feel something firm beneath me. What was Winston talking about? She was forty years old, she wasn't pretty any more, that's what he thought, she was a suburban housewife, she wasn't sophisticated enough. There must be someone else, someone younger, bustier, someone different. The new house, angry neighbors, she was forty, there was Ricky, she couldn't

23

manage alone, she would be so lonesome, she was forty, who would have her now? He meant it, though, she knew he meant it. Her shaking would not stop.

Chapter Three

"Meredith, you okay? If you're cold, you should go inside, I can do the rest."

For reasons Meredith did not entirely understand, Alex was here on a Wednesday evening, helping her shovel her own personal load of snow at the new Meredith Bennett abode in west Wilmette. She paused to flex her fingers, frozen and painful in inadequate gloves. Five years ago, back when she was Mrs. Dr. Alexander Bennett, Meredith would borrow her husband's L.L. Bean gloves to clear the flagstone walk to their Kenilworth home. Her fingers stuck out like toasty sausages as she cursed his absence – another late night at the hospital, leaving her to deal with heaps of snow and the care and feeding of their two small daughters, after her own long work day as an assistant state's attorney at the Skokie Courthouse. But how could you argue that someone who was saving lives should be at home slinging snow and zapping fish sticks? Eventually Alex had confessed that he was saving lives only 75 percent of the evening shift. During the remaining 25 percent, he was performing mouth-to-mouth on Shawna, the 24-

year-old receptionist who was now the new, improved Mrs. Alexander Bennett.

"I'm okay," she said, straightening her wire-rimmed glasses and tucking a stray brown curl under her hat. "My hands are just cold."

Meredith was close to the garage, while Alexander, near the street, manfully hacked at the icy barrier the snowplow had pushed back into the driveway. Meredith had gladly relinquished that part of the job to Alex when he had arrived early for their coffee date. She shouldn't say date, this was not a date. They were simply two concerned parents meeting to discuss their child at a local coffee shop. Wiggling her fingers, Meredith admired Alexander's thrusts and tosses, his once twinge-inducing musculature concealed under a familiar herringbone coat encrusted with snow. Despite his fancy cottage-on-steroids in Kenilworth and his ridiculous new wife, Alex still wore the same clothes that he had worn since he had first started working as a doctor fourteen years ago, when they got married. And, yes, the same old gloves. Her glasses started to fog up from her own warm breath.

"Hi, Mrs. Bennett. Are you ready for me?" Hurrying past Alex, Abby Fisher leaped over a snow heap and skidded toward the front door. She and her sister Kelsey had helped their mother clear the afternoon snow from their walk and driveway across the street like good, well brought-up children, not like her own spoiled little moochers. At age twelve, Maggie ought to be helping now, but getting her outside was a painful process, and ultimately fruitless in terms of the amount of snow she actually removed, what with the constant adjustments to her clothing and her pauses to sigh and gaze absently into space. Lucy, age ten, would lope delightedly for three minutes and then announce that she had frozen to death. But Meredith knew she wasn't being a good mother. A good mother would make them shovel as part of their Family Responsibility, no matter how irritating the chore for everyone involved.

"Thanks for coming, Abby. We'll be leaving in a minute. I'll take you inside."

Meredith and Abby walked down the short, cleared path to the front door. They stomped their feet and then entered the small foyer, where Meredith took off her boots and Abby her shoes. Teenagers didn't wear boots, Maggie had announced while rejecting her own, and this was corroborating evidence. It didn't matter how deep the snow drifts or how biting the wind, being cool was more important than being cold. Winter was temporary, but being a nerd was, apparently, forever.

Climbing two carpeted steps to the living room, Meredith glimpsed Maggie and Lucy perched on the green striped loveseat bought specially for the sunroom in this, their new house. They had moved from a modest split-level in Skokie six months ago, in time to start the school year in their new elementary and junior high schools. Although watching TV, the girls glanced up to greet their babysitter. Meredith they did not register.

"Hi, Abby, it's so funny, you want to watch?" asked Lucy, chuckling as she twirled her curly side ponytail.

"Sure. Hi, Maggie."

Her eyes round with admiration, Maggie seemed to be absorbing every aspect of Abby's appearance into her own database. Meredith had to admit that Abby did exude seasoned teenaged chic, from her old man tee shirt to her gray sweat pants with "SENIOR" stamped across the butt.

"We're just going for coffee, it shouldn't be more than an hour or so. Thanks a lot for keeping the girls company," said Meredith.

"No problem. Have fun."

"Bye bye." Meredith leaned over Lucy, who promptly kissed her on the lips. Maggie lifted her hand in a don't-you-dare motion that Meredith decided to interpret as a wave. She hurried back to her boots, reassembled herself, and stepped outside to join her ex-husband.

"Okay, the kids are set. Corner Bakery?" Meredith walked toward Alexander, who had just finished flipping snow clods onto the parkway.

"Sure, that sounds good. I like their lemon bars." He started to walk toward his Mercedes.

Meredith flinched. There was no way she was getting in that car, no way she was sitting in Shawna's seat, smelling of her inimitable combination of musk, ovulation, and Britney Spears. "I'll drive," she said.

"And the lemon bar is my treat, a thank you for shoveling. I wasn't expecting that."

"My pleasure."

Alexander flashed his charmer smile, the one formerly reserved for cocktail parties and hospital trustee dinners, definitely not the expression that had greeted her after ten married years of dishes and dry cleaning and baby wipes. He folded himself into the front seat of Meredith's Honda. Buckling her seatbelt, she loosened the knot of her winter scarf, a safety precaution to prevent accidental strangulation during a car accident. Did everyone calculate the potential for death by winter outerwear? Meredith didn't know, but she wasn't taking chances. She crept along the slick road toward the anonymity of Old Orchard Shopping Center, away from her local Wilmette Starbucks, where her new neighbors might see her and Alex in operation and make much, much more of this than it was.

"Hey, it was nice shoveling together. Like old times," he said.

"Hmmph."

Meredith discreetly swallowed the retort that had been forming in her throat and glanced at Alex. He appeared to be fondly reminiscing. And despite the fact that she knew that it wasn't true, that he had never helped her, the fact that he wanted it to have been true meant something. "We're here."

She stopped the car, and they slogged through the parking lot into the heat of the Corner Bakery. Meredith never knew where to stand. Customers cued up for salad behind the sandwich people, and if you just wanted a lemon bar could you dodge around them? As an assistant state's attorney, she wanted to follow the rules, and she certainly didn't want to make anyone angry. When people felt they had been treated unfairly, they could become abusive or even violent, as Meredith well knew from her line of work. But fortunately, all was quiet here on this wintry evening. They slipped unimpeded to the baked goods counter, where Meredith ordered an oatmeal cookie and felt virtuous, because the cheesecake brownie looked so much more delicious. They took their treats and paper cups of coffee to an isolated table and sat.

"So, what's this about?" Alex asked. "You said it was something about Maggie?"

As Alexander removed his coat, Meredith caught her breath. His chest under the crisp button-down shirt still caught at her heart, and she resisted the impulse to crush her face against it, to sink into his warmth and his safety. But he wasn't safe, not for her. Observing his hands surgically slicing the lemon bar into bite-sized pieces, her eyes clamped onto the thick platinum wedding band on his left hand and felt the naked space on her own corresponding finger. For months after their divorce four years ago, she had felt the absence of her ring like a phantom limb. Now she rarely noticed it.

"Well, I just want you to know about this, since she's pretty upset. Maggie's adjustment to Wilmette

Junior High has been fine, considering that, socially, seventh grade is the armpit of the universe. A couple of girls have been friendly to her, and she particularly likes this Stacy, she may have mentioned her to you?"

"Yeah, she sounds familiar."

Gazing at him quizzically to see if he really remembered or was just humming along, Meredith noticed a small blob of lemon goo stuck to Alexander's lip, his thick lower lip that had once felt so warm and yielding against her firm, thin lips. She could just reach up and brush it off, but that way danger lay. Five years ago she would have wiped his face with casual amusement at his enthusiastic eating. But now it would be an act of such intimacy, at least for her, that she didn't dare. She should have talked to him over the phone. She would have too, but he had wanted to meet. Alex had wanted to see her, alone and face-to-face.

"Alex." She tapped her own lip pointedly and continued. "Anyway, for months, Maggie has been sitting with Stacy at lunch, hanging out at recess, and going to the mall with her, all that good stuff. But Maggie says that lately, Stacy has decided she wants to 'get into the cool group,' which apparently does not include Maggie. So Stacy sits with them at lunch, and if Maggie tries to sit, Stacy says that she's saving the seat for someone else." Meredith could picture Maggie, standing spurned in the cafeteria with her loaded tray, spinning around to view tables packed with the backs of shunning twelve-year-olds, and now forced to sit isolated in some lonely corner. Her heart broke, she could feel it in her chest, to know that every day her daughter faced this humiliation and sadness. And to her infinite gratitude, she could see that Alex felt it too. He stopped eating, set his fork down, and laid his bare right hand over her bare left hand.

His cell phone rang, and he pulled his hand back. "Sorry, just a second."

"It's okay." Meredith stood to fill her cup with more decaf. When she returned, Alex seemed agitated.

"Shawna, "I'll be home when I get there, there's a problem with Maggie. No, it's not life-threatening, but she's my daughter, Meredith and I need to… we're at the Corner Bakery for god's sake. There's nothing to be scared of, you're in Kenilworth. I'll be home soon." Alex hung up.

"It sounds like you need to go home. Look, it's okay, I just wanted to let you know what was going on with Maggie, so you could be sensitive when you see her. I don't think there's much practical we can do, just love her a little more."

Alex met her eyes. "I really don't think I could love her any more. She's our daughter." He rushed on. "Maybe Shawna could take her some place special – shopping or something, and they could talk a little. Shawna's good with Maggie, and I'm sure she can sympathize."

Well, I'm sure she can too, Meredith thought, since she was just in junior high three years ago. But it was true, Shawna was good with Maggie, both the girls loved being with her. Loved her, they all loved her.

"That sounds like a plan," Meredith said briskly, standing up. She busied herself clearing her paper dishes, putting on her winter clothes, her coat and scarf and hat, keeping her head down so that Alex could not see her face. What had she expected – what on earth had she expected?

As they walked toward the car, Meredith felt Alex's firm gloved hand on her arm. "It's slippery out here, and I know you're a little klutzy," he said. It was a joke they had, one of those married things that wasn't very funny, but which somehow sent them into ripples of laughter as it was repeated over the years. He led her to the driver's side of the car and moved his hand to her back, forcing her to face him. "Meredith, I really wanted to see you. I know it's selfish, I know I don't have any right to say this – but I miss you."

"I miss you too," she said. It sounded automatic, but it wasn't, not at all. It cost her a lot to admit it, and he didn't deserve it, but it was true. She missed him whenever she had a problem with the girls, or when they did something funny or amazing or beautiful that only he would appreciate as much as she did. She missed him because they would always be parents together. And she missed telling him the minutia of her day, the mundane stories of scruffy defense lawyers and spacey defendants and patient judges. And she missed him at night, when she ate her bowl of ice cream, two flavors mixed, alone in front of the ten o'clock news, right at the weather report when they had always eaten it, the treat at the end of another day of life. She missed him in her heart and her soul and her gut, all the friend things, and all the love. And just because he had slept with Shawna and lied to her and destroyed their marriage and ripped her heart out of her chest and trampled it on the ground, that didn't mean that all those other feelings stopped. They were overlaid with anger and pain and mistrust, but the love and longing were still there. She was afraid they would always be there.

"Have Shawna call me," Meredith said, and they got in the car and drove home.

Chapter Four

The guest room was empty. Winston must have gone to work. Pam had not seen him since yesterday's announcement, although she had heard the heavy thud of his shoes on the stairs and their steady, unperturbed march past her door late last night, when she lay sleepless in her empty bed. Now she stared at the rumpled blankets and pillows tossed to the cherry floor, thick volumes of something or another, those books he was always reading, philosophy and Greek, piled on the bedside table. Well, he would have to clean up for himself, she wasn't his maid. She wasn't his anything anymore. The mother of his child. But that didn't mean much apparently, not as much as finding the meaning of life in one of his heavy, dull books.

Cinching her pink cashmere robe tightly around her waist, she walked downstairs to the kitchen. The lake practically knocked her down, gray today and foamy, powerful and cold, over the beach toward the glass French doors to the breakfast room. Blearily munching dry Fruit Loops, Ricky slumped on a stool at the granite island and stared at the TV. Ricky, her child, this mannish boy of broad chest and baby cheeks, the meaning of her life and her sole future companion. He hadn't talked to her in over a year, not since he had turned thirteen, except to mumble inaudible answers to her rudimentary questions – what time, what homework, where. Pam knew it was pointless to ask, she couldn't hear him, but she wouldn't give up. Maybe, if she persisted, someday he would surprise her and volunteer something, a few words she could make out, a little crumb of himself.

Ricky had no idea that his family had exploded. She had been too unhinged to muster a properly reassuring maternal tone last night, and she certainly wasn't going to tell him now, at 7:00 a.m. on a Thursday. Maybe she could avoid telling him altogether, she thought. For all the interacting they did, he might not notice Winston's absence, and, from what she could tell, he wouldn't care anyway. She poured a glass of orange juice and set it in front of him – there, she had mothered him, and he did drink a sip automatically and then stood and stomped into his sneakers without untying them.

"It's cold out today – just FYI," she ventured.

Ricky pulled on a sweatshirt and stared into space.

"Honey, do you have gloves?"

"Wha – what?"

36

The doorbell rang. The snowplow service had cleared the driveway last night, and now the carpool was here, one of a set of rotating moms who drove their freshmen boys up Sheridan Road to New Trier. Ricky slung his backpack over his shoulder and stumbled to the door. Pam followed behind to lean out and wave her gratitude to whomever it was today, Lisa Meade, she thought.

"Thank you," she mouthed, waving, as Ricky flopped into the Land Rover. Lisa Meade looked away and accelerated down the circular drive to the street. That damned beach house, Pam thought.

She shut the door. Turning toward the kitchen, she felt her stomach sicken – no breakfast today, not even some blenderized fruit and yogurt to provide positive energy before yoga. There wasn't enough liquefied food in the world to give her positive energy today. Winston was leaving her – yes, by stages, he had only made it down the hall – but she knew he would follow through. It was only a matter of time before he left her for a Chicago bachelor pad and "philosophy" – Suzy Philosophy, more likely, with a great big chest. Agitated, Pam climbed the stairs and yanked stretchy items out of her bureau. She eased them over various body parts, snapped a scrunchy around her hair, and then headed to the fabulous master bathroom. The double mirror reflected the lake, filling her background with its angry slosh, its insistent ebbing and flowing rhythm. In the forefront stood a skinny, aging, rejected woman, her face gaunt and shadowed with sleeplessness, her breasts flat under an incongruously bright racerback tank top. Too bad -- it was too bad, wasn't it? She smeared on some lip gloss, and the phone rang.

"Hello." Pam held the receiver lightly, at a distance, as if it were hot.

"Tell your husband that he'd better not build that beach house. This is a warning."

"Who is this?" Pam's voice rose.

"Just tell him. Or you'll both be sorry."

The man hung up. What a coward, that was ridiculous. This was Wilmette, a place of petitions and zoning board hearings, not some mafia movie. Well, if he thought he could shake her up today, he would just have to get in line.

She hurried downstairs, grabbed her purse and her jacket and headed to the Lexus. Last year it had a red bow on its roof, like in TV commercials. Happy Birthday from Winston, thanks for nothing. Backing up jerkily, she skidded on an ice patch and then bolted forward, around the circular drive, and onto the slushy street.

Winston was leaving her, for some floozy, with a fourteen-year-old mute and a backyard everyone wanted to fire bomb. Well, maybe she'd just tear out the beach house foundation with her own bare hands, she was mad enough to do it, she had never wanted the damn thing, it was an eyesore and no mistake. To tell the truth, she never wanted the whole stupid fake villa, it was cold by the lake, and the houses were too far apart and the neighbors were mean. Had anyone welcomed them to the neighborhood when they moved in last December – had a single person brought a casserole or a poinsettia or even a box of Entenmann's doughnut holes? No ho, all they got was menacing phone calls and cold stares. They had built an amazing house that raised everyone's property values, and was anyone the least bit grateful? No! And were they tearing down their beach houses? No! Well, screw them and the horse they rode in on, screw everyone she knew.

Pam braked at the four-way stop on Lake Avenue and then spurted mechanically toward her yoga class. Damn, the traffic was backed up at the train tracks, those stupid trains came every five seconds at rush hour, rush three hours more like, and then you could never get across, gates up, gates down, lights flashing. Everything stopped for trains, sweeping men to their important jobs downtown, while her life just ticked by. But who cared about her life, what did she matter? A stupid, gigantic black Suburban loomed in front of her, blocking her view. She would just sneak around it, who the heck needed a car that big, it was unconscionable, what did they have, ten kids and a load of lumber, they should be shot. Some child was driving it, good grief, so selfish, he could wipe out entire families and emerge from the wreckage without a scratch. And of course, ding ding ding, there goes the bell and the lights, another train.

Suddenly, Pam realized that her car was on the train tracks. And a train was coming.

She felt an instant adrenaline rush, and then, oddly, a feeling of peace came over her, the feeling she strove to experience at the end of every yoga class, but which she could never quite achieve. Maybe this was the solution, the answer to everything. Nobody loved her, nobody even liked her, and everything felt so overwhelming, and she didn't know what to do. But if she just sat here….

"Lady, lady, open the door, get out of the car, hurry up!"

A teenager in a knit cap pulled urgently at her door and shouted, pounding his other fist on the window.

"Oh my god!" Pam opened the door, and he grabbed her arm and they both hurtled down the slope and away from the huge iron monster inexorably bearing down on her car, her future, her life. She staggered to her feet, her eyes wide, her body shaking. What on earth had she done? Now, on top of everything else, she would have to call State Farm.

Chapter Five

"So, where do you want to shop?" Nicole stepped out of the Camry driver's seat and tugged her scarf more tightly around her neck. It was freezing out here in the wilds of Skokie, with no warming lake breeze to raise the temperature into double digits. She stared up at the giant metal apple on top of the Old Orchard food court and prayed that the twins would move their butts out of the car so that she could lock the doors and start running.

"You look stupid in that hat, Abby, take it off." Peering through the window, Nicole could see Kelsey bent over the back seat and trying to snatch a wool cap off her sister's head.

"Leave me alone, what do you care, that stupid Turtle Fur doesn't even cover your ears. You're going to freeze in the parking lot, at least I'll be alive." Abby whacked at her sister's hands.

"You look like a logger. Look, there's Freddy!" Kelsey opened the front door and waved maniacally, as Abby huddled behind the seat.

Nicole opened the back door. "There's no one there, Abby, come out. Kelsey, leave your sister alone. You'd think you guys were two years old, not seventeen-year-old high school seniors."

Still pawing each other, Abby and Kelsey scuffled toward Marshall Fields, as Nicole raced ahead to the front door. This was shaping up to be a swell, as in rhymes-with-hell, shopping trip. But how many more of these would Nicole get? Abby and Kelsey would graduate in a few months -- then, in all likelihood, off to Amherst/K.U., respectively, and that would be the end of the shopping-for-the-prom portion of their relationship. And, as her husband Michael would undoubtedly observe, this Old Orchard adventure was a huge perk of her current stay-at-home mom status. If Nicole were still a Winters & Early partner, she would only now be boarding the train for home, her brain whizzing with the day's negotiations and discussions of complex legal strategies. Once she arrived (at the lakefront house), she would have to respond to urgent voicemail messages begging for her expertise on issues in high profile cases showcased in *The New York Times* and *The Wall Street Journal*. Instead, she now could spend quality time with her daughters, watching them pull each other's hair.

They congregated in the Fields lobby, near the perfume and make-up. "Well, Lord & Taylor has nice dresses. Why don't we start there," Nicole piped brightly.

Kelsey rolled her eyes. "Mom. Get real. That store is for old ladies. Anyway, what we need is a sports shop."

Nicole didn't want to do it, this way insanity lay, but she knew she had to ask. "Okay, I give up. Why do we need to go to a sports shop for Turnabout?"

"Jeez, Mom, sometimes I don't even know where you've been." Kelsey rolled her eyes. "Only freshmen, maybe sophomores, wear fancy dresses to Turnabout. As seniors, we are totally over that." Kelsey glanced at Abby conspiratorially. Abby looked puzzled. "Well, maybe I forgot to tell you both, but our group has been batting around some theme ideas. Last night we decided on Tennis Players and Their Ball Girls."

This was not happening. The concept of Turnabout was bad enough – some Fifties notion that girls asking boys to a dance was an inversion of the proper world order – but she had not clawed her way to the pinnacle of the Winters litigation department, Gloria Steinem and Bella Abzug had not burned their bras, for this. Nicole squinted at Kelsey, to see if she were kidding. She wasn't.

"That's ridiculous. You can't want to degrade yourselves like that. You are two intelligent women about to go to college, you are not some boys' ball girls, I can't even think about it. Let's see what they've got here, in the junior department. Let's go."

"Fine. But don't you want Abby to be cool for a change? I'm telling you, she's going to look like an idiot if she is wearing some prom dress for this. And I am shopping for myself ALONE."

Nicole forged ahead, with the twins trailing resentfully behind her. At least Kelsey was resentful, Abby was strangely silent. Thirty minutes later, they slumped, defeated, in the dressing room, piles of skimpy, sequined, negligee-type dresses heaped around them. Shoulders drooping, Abby examined her reflection in the ill-lit mirror. A shiny scarlet nylon strip clung to every lump of her solid body. "I don't know what to do about this top," she murmured mournfully, plucking at the one place without lumps, and pushing up her glasses. Her brown hair frizzed out every which way, and goose bumps swarmed over her bare white arms.

"Honestly, I think a tennis dress would be more flattering," Kelsey pronounced from her seat on the floor in the corner.

"I hate to say it, but I think you're right," Nicole admitted, studying Abby's leg, protruding from a slit in the side of what seemed to constitute the current thinking in appropriate evening wear for teenage girls. Was it any wonder that girls got pregnant in high school? She was just surprised they didn't die of exposure first. "Well, let's not give up, there are other stores. What about Saks?"

"Well, Saks is fine if you're up for spending $300. But I thought we were on a budget." Kelsey pinched her lips.

44

"Well, we are, but I want you to be happy. Abby, what do you think? This is your dress after all."

"I just want to go home. I don't look good in anything. I don't even want to go to this stupid dance." A tear slipped down Abby's cheek and settled somewhere inside her empty front.

"Oh, don't give up, Honey, you'll have fun. You're a beautiful girl, we'll find something for you. I don't care what it costs," Nicole announced recklessly.

This was all her fault, she thought. If she hadn't misbehaved at the Polynesian Resort, she would still be making the big bucks. The three of them could have gone to Young in Heart in Winnetka, which, granted, was the most annoying dress shop in the universe, where they brought you dresses one-by-one from some mysterious dress-producing porridge pot in the back, but where they could alter protruding tops or stuff them with padding, for a fee which she used to be able to afford. Now Abby finally had a date – yes, she had asked him herself, but he had accepted, and Abby liked him – and Nicole was living with the consequences of her mistake. Michael made a fine income as a lawyer, but with the loss of her income, she felt uncomfortable wasting hundreds of dollars on a proper dress bought where everyone else on the North Shore shopped. She was a terrible mother and a worse wife. And she missed Winters & Early, where she had haggled with fully formed adults, and success was measured in dollars and cents, not in the absence of tears. This was her penance, and no mistake.

"I just want to go home," Abby sniffed again, tugging off the monstrosity and reaching for her wooly brown sweater.

"Don't worry, Mom," Kelsey said confidentially. "I'll take her out tomorrow. We'll find something perfect, and it'll be cheap."

Somehow, Nicole took no comfort in that.

Meredith scurried across the parking lot toward The Gap. Damn, it was cold, even in her puffy down coat. Somebody ought to invent furry thigh-high boots, or maybe snow pants for adults, with a snap crotch so you could go to the bathroom. She looked up to see three hatless women clutching jackets around themselves and hurtling toward their car. Well, not everyone was as practical as she was.

"Hey, Nicole, Abby, Kelsey!" Meredith shouted, as the three women blew into her and she recognized their pink faces. "Shopping at this hour?"

"You too," observed Nicole, stamping her feet to keep warm as the twins dove into their car. "What brings you out here on a Thursday night?" she asked, glancing regretfully at the relative warmth of her driver's seat.

"Just picking up my daughters. They had dinner with their stepmother." Their wicked stepmother, she did not add.

"On the way home from work? They kept you late." Nicole looked skeptical. "I thought that was the whole point of a job like yours, decent hours."

Humph. That sounded insulting – but it was true. Meredith had placed her career on simmer, staying in the public sector and accepting only the occasional felony case, in order to spend more time with Maggie and Lucy. But she didn't need Nicole Fisher, recent Doberman law firm partner, to suggest that she was slumming. Well, it was February, maybe Nicole's brain was frozen. And people said stupid things, especially when they were unhappy themselves. Meredith didn't know the circumstances of Nicole's own step away from power into the full-time mothering of daughters who would be leaving for college in a few months. It seemed like an odd choice.

"Yeah, well – standing up for truth and justice is a big job." There, Nicole, take that, I'll bet you never sent any speeders to traffic school. "Nice that you can spend more time with the girls, now that you're an at-home mom." Actually, Meredith thought it was nice. Using the lovely Shawna, seductress of her husband and now of Maggie and Lucy, as after-school childcare, was not her notion of the ideal family arrangement.

"Yeah, well, gotta go, Meredith, it's so cold! See you later." Nicole leaped into her car, and Meredith hustled into The Gap.

"Mom, yay. Look what Shawna bought me."

Meredith's ten-year-old daughter, Lucy, ran up excitedly, her eyes shining, a chocolate smear on her cheek. She yanked a cluster of cardboards out of a plastic bag and thrust them at her mother.

"Wow, stick-on earrings." Meredith admired them and then returned them to Lucy, who was dancing a ceremonial jig of blessing to the god of cheap plastic jewelry. "Did you say thank you to Shawna?"

"Course."

Lucy took Meredith's arm and walked her through a maze of tables displaying multi-colored tee shirts and small spandex items that she hoped were undergarments. Around a corner stood Shawna, unfurling precisely folded sweaters for Maggie's appraisal. Meredith remembered the pain of being twelve years old, the desire to grow out of her chubby, hobbit body into the nymph that some girls had already become, the prayer for a miraculous growth spurt that overnight would propel her from near-sighted sphere to lithe reed in need of a trip to the bra department. She could see how Maggie might idolize Shawna, who had probably never even passed through the squatty phase, who probably emerged from the womb as a sleek, model-thin blonde in a mini skirt and fashion boots. Shawna had a talent, the ability to look feline and stylish in any situation, which Meredith neither possessed nor underestimated. Shawna's allure had stomped on Meredith's intelligence and hard work and kicked them to the curb.

Because her husband had left her for Shawna. He had taken the cheerleader's hand and leaped gleefully over his wife's still-warm body. Shawna bore some responsibility, but mostly, it was Alexander's fault. He was the one who had married her, he was supposed to be the one who saw her and loved her. And Meredith had to remember that.

"Hi Maggie, hello, Shawna. Thanks so much for taking them."

"Sure, no problem. You know I always love seeing the girls."

Actually, that seemed to be true. Shawna didn't always tell the truth, but she was always willing to babysit if Meredith had to work late, and that was a treasure beyond rubies. And after Alex had told her about Maggie's friend problems, Shawna had immediately volunteered to take the girls out for a little distracting fun. That Shawna made Meredith look like an unhip vegetable-pushing party pooper was something that she had to accept, considering the convenience and her children's glowing faces. It was good to see Maggie smiling.

"Well, we'll let you go home now," Meredith said, because she really wanted to go home herself. Maggie and Lucy immediately started trailing after their mother. They had had a full day of school and, from the looks of Lucy's face, a boatload of cheesecake, and were undoubtedly ready for pajamas.

"No rush. Alex isn't home anyway. Working late at the hospital, some infected something again. You know."

Shawna was peering into Meredith's face, trying to find the answer to the riddle of her husband. Well, Meredith was familiar with this puzzle, as was Shawna, though now the tables had turned. During all those "late nights at the hospital" that Alex had spent with Shawna back in their days of premarital bliss, she must have known that Alex was lying to his wife. And now that Alex was using that same line on Shawna, she had to wonder – was it legit or not? Alex had been spending more time with Meredith lately, strictly to discuss the children, of course, but he seemed to want to be with her these days. And Meredith did know where Alexander had been tonight, and it wasn't at the hospital, at least not the whole time. So, they had grabbed a bite of dinner after work. It was just dinner. They had to eat. And turnabout is fair play, right?

"Well, good night, Shawna, and thanks again."

"Good night," the girls chimed in. And they walked out together, Meredith and her daughters, into the icy wind between The Gap and home, as Shawna stood alone between shelves of perfectly folded jeans.

Chapter Six

In the kitchen broiling healthy salmon for two, Nicole scuffed across the linoleum in her slippers to the beat of the oldies radio station. Alarmingly, the oldies had morphed into the music of her teenage years, implying something sinister about her own rung on the ladder of life that she didn't want to face. Well, at least her music had real singers with real melodies, not like that robotic, mix-mastered pablum that Kelsey and Abby favored. Nicole chopped asparagus into bite-sized chunks and threw it in a pan with some store-bought teriyaki sauce. A key struggled in the back door lock – probably Michael, but she wasn't going to race over to let him in, she had important household tasks to perform.

"Hello."

Tilting his chilly face down for a kiss, Michael smiled, then headed to the front closet to hang his overcoat. Nicole tossed a couple placemats on the kitchen table, then squatted to open the oven door and check the salmon. Oh, she almost forgot, the secret sauce, another store-bought concoction, also sweet, which inevitably charred under the broiler and stuck to her teeth. A fumbling sound behind her indicated that Michael had quickly changed into his jeans and was now rifling through the mail.

"The girls aren't here," Nicole volunteered, turning off the rice. "Kelsey's out with Brandon, and Abby is going to Northbrook with various Laurens for last-minute Turnabout stuff. Don't ask me what, I don't even want to think about it."

"Well, they deserve a break after a full week at New Trier." Michael reached into the cupboard for two plates and started filling his.

"Well, deserve it or not, they certainly bolt on Friday nights. Kind of nice for us, though."

Nicole was not sure about this last. She liked spending time with Michael, and asking the girls how their day went was about as much fun as a root canal. But eating dinner at home with her husband alone was awkward. Sometimes she felt like she was in a box seat above the table, gazing down and cringing, while a narrator wondered aloud, "Will this marriage survive?" At least if the girls were here, there was someone else to blame for the non-sparkling dialogue.

"Pretty big news at the firm today." Michael picked up his wine glass and swirled his allotment of antioxidant-rich merlot.

"Yeah?" Oh, good, there was going to be something to talk about besides scintillating developments in the trusts and estates department and this weekend's schedule.

"Guess who's leaving the firm?" Michael gave Nicole barely three seconds to ponder before he blurted, "Winston Bigelow! He sent out a memo announcing that he was leaving the partnership 'to pursue his interest in philosophy.' Can you believe that? What a crock! I knew the guy was pretentious, but what is he up to? Nobody would leave such a lucrative job, and after all the heads he had to knock together to get there, to stare at his own navel! That guy's got to have an angle. At least he was head of litigation long enough to have racked up a boatload of money – he and his family can still live in his gaudy new house. The bastard. I'll never forgive him for tearing down our place."

Nicole had stopped chewing about a minute back. Winston was leaving the firm. And as much fun as slapping sauce on fish and answering phone calls from the twins saying they weren't coming home and closing the refrigerator with her butt while she set the table had turned out to be, maybe this was her chance. Except that Michael wouldn't understand why, and she didn't think she could tell him.

"Yuh, that is big news," she said, playing for time. "How's dinner?"

"Delicious, as usual. I love coming home to your dinners, it's great. Remember how, when you were working all the time, we used to have to scrambled eggs or eat frozen pizza ...."

This was not good, what was she thinking? She would have to regroup. "It was nice to have the extra money, though. Our old house, the beach – that was special."

Now Michael stopped chewing. "Nicole, what's going on? I thought you liked being home."

"It's fine. Never mind." She picked up a dainty bite of asparagus on the tines of her fork with what she hoped was a display of a small, private sadness.

"No, what? I'm not making enough money? Because I know that my income isn't as big as yours was, not by a long shot, but it's perfectly livable. I'm not some big honcho, but I am a partner, most people would be thrilled to make this sort of money." Michael set his fork on his plate. His cheeks flushed, and his clenched hands mirrored the tension in his face.

"No, of course not, that's not what I meant. Michael, you are a wonderful provider, and this time at home has been special. But you know I didn't quit my job by choice. We had that – problem – and you wanted me to quit, and I did. But the girls don't need me much, everyone's busy but me, and I'm not used to it. I like to be out there in the big world, interacting, thinking hard about legal problems, feeling like I matter. Sometimes I feel like a prisoner in this house. If you didn't call me every day, sometimes I wouldn't talk to anyone until four, and all I get at four is a grunt while Abby grabs a snack, heads for her room, and shuts the door. I love you, but I need more."

"Yeah, I know. I mean, I thought so. But I was hoping." He looked down dejectedly. "I hoped that I – we – would be enough for you."

Nicole reached out and stroked Michael's wrist. "Look, I know what I did. I am so sorry. I will never do anything like that again, not ever, I have learned my lesson. I am swearing off tiki bars for life." She smiled, and he struggled to smile back at her. "But I want to go back to work at Winters & Early. I think they'll have me back. The girls are going to college in a few months, it would be a financial help, and there won't be anyone here but me, just knocking around. I won't go back if you don't want me to, I will do whatever you want, but please, be okay with this."

Michael looked at his wife. "I hear you, I do, and I want you to be happy. And I do think you've changed, I don't think you'll do it again. But you'll be travelling – how can I be sure, how can I ever be sure? Maybe you've changed, but the world hasn't, and all hotels have bars, and maybe you'll just need to unwind, and there will be some other random travelling guy…."

"But that's where you're wrong, the world has changed." Nicole pushed back her plate and reached across the table to take Michael's hands. "Michael, I want to tell you something, and I don't want you to freak out." She paused. "I didn't tell you the whole truth about that night, and you'll see why, I know you'll understand. But now I think you're ready for it, now that things have taken this good turn and Winston is leaving the firm."

She stopped to gather herself. This was going to be awful, but she had started it, she had to forge ahead. And she needed her job back, and she hated leaving Michael with a false impression – who was she kidding, lying to him, she had hated lying to him for the last sixteen months.

"What does this have to do with Winston?" Michael asked slowly, trying to withdraw his hands from his wife's. She held on tight. "No. No," he said.

"I am so sorry. We were both there, in the hotel bar, and you know we were celebrating winning the Benihana case. We'd had a lot to drink."

"No. Stop. And that bastard hit on you?"

"It wasn't like that. We were talking, he was telling me about some Aristotle he was reading, and we were so drunk, and I felt so far away from my real life – this was Disneyworld for god's sake, it didn't seem real, and I don't know, I wasn't thinking, I think I might have said something or done something…."

Michael stopped listening. He knew Nicole was talking, her mouth was moving, but he didn't need to listen, he could see it all so clearly. Winston and Nicole, sitting in those basket chairs, like Morticia and Gomez Addams on TV. They both had big drinks, Nicole's flirty and girly, pink in a curvy glass with a little red parasol, and Winston's in a broad-nosed brown mug shaped like a native's head. Winston was expounding about his own importance, but really he kept glancing at Nicole's bare legs in those strappy high heels she wore on special occasions. And Nicole couldn't hear him in the basket chair, so she kept leaning forward, her slightly unbuttoned blouse catching on the edge of the chair and unbuttoning more. And then, of course, who could resist her – well, certainly Winston wouldn't even try, he was king of the world, he would just reach over and grab what he wanted and to hell with everyone else. Michael couldn't believe that Nicole had let him continue to work with Winston -- Jesus, that they had sold their house to him – he had taken Michael's wife and his home and her job, he had taken everything. And he showed no regret, no remorse, he just kept churning along.

"And I don't even know if he remembers anything – we were so drunk, and I left right away. He's certainly never said anything, it's like it never happened. And that's the thing you've got to understand, Michael. In a way, it didn't happen. We weren't ourselves, we were in some, I don't know, movie set for *Mutiny on the Bounty,* it wasn't real, none of it was real. You and I are what matters. And now that he's leaving, we can be free of all this, we can completely move on as if none of it ever happened, because really, in real life, none of it did."

Michael pushed his chair back from the table. He stood up and walked out. The front door banged. He hadn't even taken his coat.

Something about the body's reaction to shock, he didn't feel cold. That Meredith across the street had waved to him as he stormed out, she probably thought it was pretty strange, just shirt sleeves in February, but what the hell did he care what she thought, it was nobody's business but his own. He felt like the whole town had turned into an extension of his living room, more like an extension of his own head. All he could do was walk, stomping over snow heaps as he passed nameless streets and unseen houses and shops until he came after some unknown length of time to, of course, a Starbucks. His hands were stiff, he was probably freezing, but the inner furnace of his rage kept him feeling warm and toasty. This probably wasn't healthy, and he didn't know if he cared, he wasn't sure he would ever care about anything rational again. Well, maybe a double espresso would be fuel on the fire, just what he needed to set himself up for the next lap of his walk who knows where.

Michael opened the door, and damn these small towns, damn this small world, who should be sitting right across from the barista and facing his way but Pam Bigelow, boring wife of the infamous Winston. There she sat, placidly lapping up the rewards of her husband's arrogance, like the wife of Genghis Khan. Michael ordered a venti Americano and plopped down across from her. She started, then stared, as if she had been in a reverie and had no idea who he was. Well, he was only a sniveling mid-level partner, and her husband was the grand pooh bah, she probably didn't recognize him. She wouldn't forget him after this, though. He was going to rock her world.

"Pam, I'm Michael Fisher. I work at Winters with your husband." He thrust out his hand.

She nodded. "Hello. Nice to see you." She spoke automatically, but her forehead wrinkled slightly.

"So, I hear Winston is leaving the firm."

"Yes." She looked down, obviously uncomfortable, probably wishing he would leave. Fat chance.

"Look can I buy you – what, a skinny vanilla latte? You look like a skinny vanilla latte kind of girl."

She smiled slightly and looked up at him. "No thanks. I'm good."

"Well, rumor has it that Winston is leaving to become a *philosopher*." He said it like it was some kind of poisonous shrub and made a creepy woo woo motion with his fingers, brushing her forearm. She pulled back.

"Yuh. That's what he says."

"You sound like you don't believe him."

"I don't know. It's hard to believe." Pam stared into space. Michael wasn't sure she was talking to him, more like thinking out loud, working things out for herself. "But Winston doesn't lie, that would go against his principles." She brushed a few pale hairs away from her face and gazed down at the table.

"Interesting. It must be nice to live with such an upstanding guy." He paused. "But, you see, I wouldn't know. My wife, Nicole Fisher, you might know her – it turns out, she doesn't have a lot of integrity."

Pam shifted uncomfortably. "I don't know her very well, I just know she's one of his litigation partners. She doesn't talk to me. Well, she talks, she says some words, she's pleasant. Frankly, I don't know why she bothers, probably something to do with Winston. Maybe I shouldn't say that to you."

"No, no, you're very astute, amazing that you have figured out in a few brief run-ins what it took me twenty years to understand. Which is, that Nicole doesn't always tell the truth. She likes to bend it a little, or leave things out, to make it nice and digestible. But Winston – you say he always tells the truth? And by that, I mean that he tells you all of it, he doesn't omit inconvenient details, not even to spare your feelings?" Michael took a gulp of his Americano, choked, and coughed.

Pam picked up her paper cup and pushed her chair back with a rough, screeching sound. "Look – Michael – I don't know what this is, but I think I have to go now." Her left hand fluttered around, searching for her scarf.

"Okay, I'm sorry, please stay. I just really need to ask you something, to tell you something, or maybe you already know, married to such a fine gentleman as Winston. Okay, sorry."

Michael rubbed his forehead. Now that it was time to quit toying with Pam and actually tell her, it was not so easy. She looked pretty pathetic and miserable already. But she needed to know the truth. Otherwise she was being played for a fool, like he had been. It was the right thing to do. Okay, who was he kidding, it was the mean thing to do, at least that's what he was hoping. He wanted to be mean to Winston. And this Pam – well, he'd thought she was some complicit dope who put her fingers in her ears and said la la la and then reaped the financial benefits of her husband's unscrupulous behavior – but she might actually be clueless, and she might actually care. And didn't they have a kid, what about him? Well, Winston should have thought of that, this was all his fault. Michael wasn't doing anything wrong. He was just the messenger.

Pam stumbled out of Starbucks into the cold winter night. Of course she had known that Winston was leaving her for another woman. Who quits a lucrative law firm job and leaves his family to study Plato? But still, it was a shock to hear it confirmed, to hear that Winston had already cheated on her at least once, to find

61

out that her serious husband, who honestly was constantly reading books with Greek on one side of the page, was actually a big horn dog liar like all the other men in the world, that their whole marriage was just one big lie. Was Ricky actually even her son? Well, wait a minute, of course he was, but who knew how many other children Winston had lying around. She felt so special when this smart, important man married her, and he loved her, and they had a child together and a riparian house – they had a whole life, and now it meant nothing, it was gone, poof, finished. And it never even was there, he had never loved her. All those times she thought she was being adorable or sexy or interesting, the whole time he was just laughing up his sleeve and then sleeping with Nicole on business trips. No wonder Nicole looked down on Pam. She was playing Pam for a fool at work and in her husband's bed. And if Winston had lied to her, he had screwed around and never told her about it, this man who had so much integrity – well that must just mean that Pam was nothing. She didn't deserve to know anything, she was beneath his notice. She was nothing.

She was home now. She had walked all the way, and she didn't even remember crossing Sheridan Road. Every light in the house was on – Ricky must be home, and not Winston, Winston would have shut most of them off to prevent waste. Pam unlocked the front door and stepped across the threshold. She took off her coat and followed a trail of cookie crumbs to the basement, where Ricky lay under a Chicago Bears Snuggie and watched the big screen TV, while the lake lurked black on the other side of the glass door to the backyard.

"Hi, Honey. What are you watching?"

"Shmuff."

Pam didn't know why she asked. She might have thought he was playing a game with her, except he got so mad when she asked him to repeat himself. Clearly, there was a basketball game on the screen, a green team and a red one.

"Who's winning?"

"Shmuff."

That's what she thought. "Well, come up at eleven. Are you ready for Turnabout tomorrow night? I guess you'll need to pick up the corsage I ordered."

"Bushmuff."

She knew she would be picking up the corsage herself, or the poor girl wouldn't get one. Well, he was a fourteen year old boy, he didn't know how important these things were to girls, how much they wanted to feel pretty and cared for and special.

Slogging up the stairs, Pam contemplated her life, and her nose started running. Here she was, in a fancy lakefront house she didn't want, with neighbors that hated her because her soon-to-be ex-husband was a greedy, lying pig, with a son who exhibited zero interest in her and at best would be off on his own in three years. Yes, she taught yoga, but that was just to keep from going crazy with boredom and to keep her figure – well, that she had done, like anyone cared. Standing in the

63

giant master bedroom, she pressed her face against the glass door and tried to see the lake. It was too dark, but she could feel its pull, back and forth, back and forth, powerful and inevitable as death.

Chapter Seven

It was six o'clock on Saturday night, time to take the twins to stage one of the multi-event process entitled, simply, Turnabout. The experience of planning this special high school evening would prepare North Shore girls for futures as film producers, major generals, and CEO's of Fortune 500 corporations. First, they must invite a date in a unique, eye-popping way, possibly involving a hot air balloon or a Big Ten marching band formation. Reservations must be made for super-fun transportation, generally a minibus, a Chicago trolley, or a stretch limousine large enough to hold twenty-six over-stimulated teenagers and rented for long enough to drive them to dinner at a downtown restaurant, back to Winnetka for the dance, and then to the afterparty. If the initial picture party and the afterparty were in different places, plans must be made to have casual clothing, sleeping bags, and transportation home waiting at the second location. Each group, especially of juniors and seniors, needed a clever, preferably degrading or quasi-obscene theme, and appropriate clothes and flowers must be procured. Many of the girls had their hair and nails professionally groomed, although Kelsey and Abby skipped this step due to current family austerity measures. The whole ordeal began with the picture party, at which parents dotingly snapped photos of their children, dates, and friends as if they were Hollywood celebrities. None of this was ever easy on the parents, but tonight promised to be harder than usual for Nicole.

"Girls, are you ready?" she shouted up the stairs. Resisting the urge to check herself out in the hall mirror, Nicole reached for the camera and her shoes.

Cautious clicking noises culminated in the twins' arrival in the living room. Although Nicole had been around the block a few times with New Trier dances with Kelsey, her daughters' doublemint appearance tonight constituted a dazzling new low.

"Okay," she said, performing an Oscar-winning impression of a calm person, "what are you supposed to be?"

Abby and Kelsey were dressed alike, although dressed was an exaggeration. They sported black plastic bags cinched at the waist with duct tape, and with holes cut at appropriate junctures for their head and arms to jut through. The head hole seemed particularly large and ill-conceived, allowing, in Kelsey's case, for a thrilling display of cleavage, and in Abby's, for a puzzling view of flat white skin. They wore fishnet stockings on their legs, and, oddly, on their arms as well. Both also displayed large quantities of sparkly blue eye shadow and red lip gloss and wore dangerous spiky high heels.

"The theme is sanitation workers and their trash. We're the trash," Kelsey announced, grinning.

"So I see," said Nicole. "Shouldn't you at least get to be the sanitation workers, its being Turnabout and all?"

"That's what I thought," said Abby. "But none of the girls wanted to wear an orange cotton jumpsuit."

"Understandable – that certainly wouldn't be flattering," said Nicole. It was too late now, she thought. In a few months the girls would be in college, and she wouldn't have to see any of this. Oddly, this thought was a relief, despite the fact that her blissful oblivion would not eliminate the probability that they would be doing this and worse when she wasn't around to see it. "Well," she sighed. "Let me take a couple pictures before we go."

The girls posed in front of the fireplace. "Where's Dad?" Kelsey asked.

"Umm, he had to go to work," Nicole lied. Michael's absence constituted special difficulty number one for Nicole, not counting the trash bags. Because after last night's revelation that Winston had been her partner – well, more than her partner – in the unfortunate Polynesian Resort incident, Michael had returned home only briefly. He had collected his coat and his car and then driven away without a word to her. She had so hoped that he would resurface to talk things through, or at least to support Abby on her big night. Nicole doubted that he would show up later for the picture party, due to extra difficulty number two. In a weird incidence of karma, of fate's waves washing back and giving her what she deserved, that gathering was being held at Winston and Pam Bigelow's house.

"Okay, get your coats."

"Mom, we don't need coats. There's no place to put them, we'll just lose them at the dance," said Kelsey, opening the back door to admit a gasp-inducing blast of February wind.

"Couldn't you leave them on the bus?"

"Whatever," said Kelsey, as Abby grabbed hers and zipped it up tight.

"What about this watch-the-sun-rise-over-the-lake business? Do you plan to that in just your trash bags?" Nicole shut the door. It was starting to snow.

"Oh, yeah, our stuff," said Abby, and she ran back into the house and returned carrying two crammed backpacks. "We've got clothes to change into at the afterparty. That's at the Bigelows' too, so we can just leave our junk there."

They walked to the car, Abby lugging the backpacks, and Kelsey clutching her dress to keep it from flying into a tree. Fluttering sideways, the snow did look pretty, before it gusted into white squalls that stung Nicole's face and clung to her blue knitted cap. Ahead of her, Abby skidded in her stilettos on the icy cement of their backyard walkway. This whole evening was such a terrible idea, Nicole didn't even know where to start.

She tried to make her mind a quiet blank space, like the roof of the garage.

"How did the Bigelows end up with these two parties anyway?" Nicole asked, as they settled in the car.

"Just lucky," grinned Kelsey. "Actually, that was me."

"What are you talking about?" Nicole slowly backed the car into the alley. She turned on the windshield wipers and hit various defrost buttons as well as her neighbor's garbage cans. Just a tap.

"I told Ricky Bigelow that we always had those parties at our house before his father tore it down, and that it was so cool to have everybody there, by the lake and everything, so he said we could still come to his house. I mean, I know it's freaky, since he's a freshman and we're seniors, but it'll be kind of awesome too. I miss the old place."

"This isn't exactly the old place," noted Abby, as they pulled past the gigantic Tuscan villa that filled their old lot. A minibus throbbed in the cobblestone circular drive, in front of the double front doors. Every light in the house was on, and snow stuck to the green tile roof. The whole place sparkled like a Hollywood set that fell off a truck on its way to Universal Studios Orlando. Lord help us, I hope Michael doesn't show up, Nicole thought, as she shuffled behind her skidding children into the mansion of the possibly amnesiac man who had impulsively ruined her life.

So, they were having a fancy party at the Bigelow place, clogging up his quiet cove with Expeditions and Grand Cherokees, just the kind of gargantuan gas guzzlers you would expect from a family with no concern for their neighbors or the environment. And of course they hadn't invited him, he only lived next door. From the parked-up look of things, Mr. Important Winston Bigelow hadn't invited anyone on the entire stretch of Michigan Avenue, not even in some sleazy attempt to ingratiate himself. Still. He tugged on his dog's leash and shuffled cautiously down the icy sidewalk.

"Come along, Angus."

Ned Haskell had lived on Michigan Avenue in Wilmette – on the lake side – for over thirty years. A lifetime ago, his two children, Nancy and Bill, had played in the backyard sand for endless hours with their plastic buckets and shovels. They had built castles and towns and rivers, and they had splashed in the clear water and used their imaginations. In those days, kids didn't need expensive electronics to have fun, just a little mesh bag of cheap toys from the Five and Dime. That was before the invasion of the new people, with their blight of beach houses, wrecking the view up and down the lake, turning it into some kind of shanty town near the water. Ned and his wife Eileen would never have dreamed of cluttering up the lakeshore's natural beauty with some extravagant heap of brick and cement. Sure, Nancy and Bill had tracked a little sand and water into the house every day, but this was beach living, for Pete's sake, and Eileen didn't mind cleaning it up. It was a small price to pay for the magic of having the lake in your backyard. Most folks in Wilmette owned tidy parcels of land just wide enough for a house and a garage and a few feet of fence neatly lined with hostas and shrubbery. But behind his house, thirty years ago, back in the late Sixties – heck, even in the Seventies and Eighties -- you could take in an uninterrupted view of sand and dune grasses, up and down for blocks in each direction. His old neighbors might throw down a lawn chair or two, but that was it. That world was gone now, destroyed by a few selfish big spenders. And now the Bigelows were the topper on the cake, with the showiest beach house, closest to the water, of all.

Ned paused next to a large brick pillar marking one end of the Bigelows' circular drive. The driveway was made out of rounded pavers, like cobblestones, a sure sign that Winston Bigelow had more money than he knew what to do with. Ned peered nervously around the pillar – you never knew when one of these self-centered crazies would peel out and crush you or Angus, Ned's friendly miniature collie. But the driveway was quiet, except for a minibus parked by the front doors with, of course, its engine running, and a very untrustworthy uniformed female dozing in the driver's seat. Why did they need a bus – to ferry them and their drunken friends on some expensive junket? Well, they had better watch themselves, Ned was this close to calling the police. And he knew other neighbors, less understanding than himself, who might consider all of this the last straw, who might take matters into their own hands and end the Bigelows' reign of terror once and for all.

Ned was not a violent man, but some folks just didn't listen to reason. The neighborhood association – well, a few concerned citizens who got together every once in a while to talk about how the street had gone downhill -- had tried talking to Bigelow and his wife, they had tried warning them, they had even tried to scare them with a few sinister phone calls and the threat of bad publicity. Nothing seemed to have any effect. The Bigelows had no shame, and every day a few more layers of brick were added to the eyesore in the back. Ned would have burned it down himself, and he knew others who would have joined him, but the thing was built like a bunker, they would have to blow it up. And they were all old gray-haired guys, unaccustomed to handling explosives. Most likely they would end up incinerating themselves – and then who would have the last laugh?

A few scantily clad teenage girls walked past. They were giggling and wobbling, their shoes way too tall, and their dresses – were those even dresses? – way too short for this February weather. Didn't these girls have parents? And what was going on in that house anyway, some obscene shot-guzzling party where old geezers procured young girls to fulfill their unspeakable desires? Eileen would turn in her grave if she knew what her beloved neighborhood had come to. This just couldn't go on. He was going to have to step out of his comfort zone and take decisive, drastic action, to stop these Bigelows once and for all. He didn't know yet what he would do, but he was on Neighborhood Watch late tonight, he would be patrolling the lakefront area in the cold quiet under the stars. It would be a good time to think it all through. Surely something would dawn on him.

Suddenly, Ned stopped. What was going on -- something was choking him. He grabbed at his neck and felt his too-tight scarf and scrabbled with his fingers to loosen it. Just ahead, Angus jerked excitedly toward a squirrel, the fringed ends of the scarf dangling damply from his mouth.

"Angus, let go!" Ned yanked his tail, and the dog released it from his teeth. Shaken, Ned rummaged in his pocket for his key and led himself and Angus into the relative safety and quiet of their house.

All Ricky could think about was his X-Box. If only he could just, like, sneak down the basement stairs, flop down on that long, loungy part of the sofa, and grab his controller, he might still be able to have a fun night. Why did that Flora girl have to ask him to Turnabout, and why did his parents have to make him say yes? He didn't like this junk, it was boring and exhausting. He just wanted to curl up and disappear.

"Freshmen young ladies," some dorky dad called out, and all the girls ran in front of the fireplace in the living room to pose, while their parents madly snapped photos like they were paparazzi or something, all those flashing lights and all that smiling and hamming it up. Ricky could hardly stand to look at the girls, mostly because he wanted to stare at them. Dealing with them at school was hard enough, when they were dressed in tight tee shirts and clingy pants that didn't meet in the middle. Now they were wearing shiny, short dresses with low-cut tops and spiky shoes, like they were leaking out of both ends of a Chinese finger puzzle. Pinning that rose thing on Flora's shirt was one of the most humiliating things he had ever done in his life. He had to figure out how to grab a clump of the fabric without sticking a pin in her or feeling her up, and his mother was taking pictures the whole time like they were three years old and in preschool. But this was his life, he was going to have to sit by this girl and talk to her and dance with her, and she was going to tell her friends every dumb thing he did and make up a few extras besides. And he had to wear this stupid outfit, a jacket and real shoes and a belt. He couldn't even believe it. This was the worst day of his life, and it was all his parents' fault.

His father was certainly enjoying himself. Everybody was admiring his fancy house, or at least everybody who didn't live in the neighborhood. That was what they were saying anyway, but Ricky thought they were overdoing it. Their mouths were hanging open and they were going in all the rooms and touching stuff, like they were trying to figure out how much it all cost. He knew that most kids from Wilmette didn't live like this, they had normal houses with worn-out furniture and backyards with swing sets and old sand boxes, not whatever this was, mansions with big beaches and marble fireplaces. At least it was dark so they couldn't see the beach house going up. Ricky didn't know what the big deal was, but he knew people hated it, he had even answered a few crank calls himself.

His parents were putting on a good show, they were a couple of fine actors, somebody ought to call the Academy Awards. His mother was zipping around the kitchen island, checking the silver coffeepot thing and filling the bucket with fresh ice cubes. The dining room table was covered with food that nobody was eating, lots of shrimp and vegetables with sauce and some kind of mini pieces of bread that she was really excited about. If she had put out potato chips or brownies, the boys would have totally gorged themselves, but boys didn't eat this cute healthy junk, and the girls never ate anything as far as he could tell. They probably went home and snarfed down the refrigerator, like animals with vacuum cleaners for noses. And his father was showing everybody his paintings and explaining about his collection of Incan pottery, which filled all the bookshelves in the living room and hallway. He didn't bother to add that he was sleeping in the guest room and moving out next week. It didn't matter at all to Ricky, he totally didn't care if his father lived or died, but he knew his mother was upset, even though she tried to hide it. They actually hadn't told him anything, but he had eyes and ears, and if they thought he didn't know things, then they were stupider even than he thought they were.

Kelsey's mom, Mrs. Fisher, was talking to his dad now. She was kind of a fox, except she could stand to put on a little make-up or something, maybe some jewelry or a clean shirt. But she was pretty like Kelsey, just old. That didn't seem to slow Winston down, he was yucking it up, giving her a wink, like they had a secret or something. Mrs. Fisher looked a little shocked, and she grabbed his dad's arm and clung on to it.

Kabbamm! Across the family room, Ricky's mom dropped a whole tray of wine glasses, and she was staring at Winston and Mrs. Fisher. Now all the parents were diving around, falling all over themselves trying to clean up. Somebody even made a joke about having the senior boys use the senior girls' dresses, pretty hilarious actually if it weren't so embarrassing. His mother looked like she was going to cry, and he totally hoped she wouldn't, that was the last thing he needed. Maybe if he ducked down behind a chair or went to the bathroom, this would all blow over. The only adult who didn't seem to care was Winston. That was typical. He always let everybody else pick up the pieces.

"So, the kids are coming back here, hanging out, and then going over to the beach?" Some clueless dad behind him was asking somebody else's mom.

"Yup, that's the plan. I'm not thrilled about it, but what can you do? I guess that's what everyone does, so you can't really say no. At least the party's not at our house. And I'm sure the Bigelows will keep an eye on them. What could go wrong?"

They both laughed. Ricky felt like popping up and telling them that his parent weren't even speaking to each other, and even if they were, they didn't care what he did. And if they didn't care about him, they certainly didn't give a crap about somebody else's kids. Anybody over here tonight had total license to run wild. To some people, that would be a great party. But Ricky just wanted to go to bed. Or murder his jerk dad. One or the other.

Chapter Eight

This was the third time this week, and it was getting to be a habit. Once Shawna had known, once she hadn't, and now, on Saturday night, Meredith neither knew, nor cared what she thought. As ugly as it seemed in a certain light, Shawna was performing the appropriate task – she was babysitting for Maggie and Lucy while their parents went out on a date. The fact that said parents were not married to each other, but that one was in fact married to the babysitter, was the result of a bend in the universe or demonic possession. That Alex seemed to be performing his own exorcism should not make Meredith feel guilty. And if he had cast her in the role of skimpily costumed contortionist assistant, what then? Well, she was properly, though carefully dressed, and a girl had to eat – so what! Alex had his daughters this weekend, he had worked a little late, they were having a quiet dinner in a downtown restaurant where hopefully no one they knew would bump into them – what was so bad about that?

"May I offer you a dessert menu?" A waiter in a black tee shirt, black leather jacket, and black string tie, sidled up to their secluded corner table and began clearing their dinner plates. Meredith had eaten a stack of halibut piled on top of a few beans, then topped with a sprinkling of brussel sprout leaves and three cubes of chopped pork belly, next to a tablespoon of couscous, all swimming in a buttery sauce that tasted faintly of licorice. She had ordered the fish to watch her calories, but the waistband of her black pants was starting to choke off the blood supply to her brain. Alex, looking sleek and masterful, was gazing at her from behind the last bites of a large, fatty steak with a side of mashed potatoes.

"Meredith?"

"Well, I'll just take a look." The waiter left, to return a moment later with two embellished cards. "I couldn't eat another bite, but I just want to see what they have."

Alex browsed the card. "Oh, look, an apple tart with cinnamon ice cream – I know you love that. And a warm chocolate lava cake with coconut ice cream – Meredith, I know you want it, you just don't think you should. It's okay, you know – you look great, you're always so careful – it's time to treat yourself. You deserve some fun." He grinned broadly.

Wait a minute, was he talking about dessert, or – what? He reached toward her and laid his open hand on the table. She straightened up. Had she really drunk half a bottle of wine? Her face felt flushed. She looked down to make sure her cashmere sweater was still on, then rolled up her sleeves. It was awfully hot in here.

The waiter came back. "We'll share the lava cake and a couple of cappuccinos," Alex ordered authoritatively. "I'm sure I can entice you into a few bites," he said to her.

I'm sure you can, Meredith thought, starved as I am. And she could see how the illicit nature of this occasion gave it a frisson of eroticism that was wonderful and compelling and electric. This was what it felt like to fall in love, it was the best part of being alive. She mustn't shut herself off out of fear of being wrong or being hurt. This feeling should be nurtured and protected, she should cup her hands around it like the flame of a votive candle, she should let its warmth and glow fill her with light. Alex's outstretched hand still lay on the table. She put hers on top of it.

"Alex," she said.

"Don't say anything," he said. "Just let it happen."

"But, Shawna." She tried to pull her hand away, but he caught hold and clutched her fingertips.

"Shhh." He reached across and put his finger on her lips. "You worry too much."

"Shouldn't we have a real conversation?" she asked.

"Not yet," he said. "Look, here's dessert."

The waiter set the chocolaty mound between them, with an upside-down spoon on each side.

Whipped cream rosettes punctuated four corners of the plate, each flower crowned with a perfect raspberry. In chocolate syrup, piped around the plate, were the words, "Be My Valentine." Meredith's eyes filled with tears.

"I know it's a little late," Alex said.

"What does it mean?" asked Meredith.

"You're such a lawyer," Alex said teasingly, and he dipped his finger into his cappuccino foam and dabbed it on her nose. She felt his knee under the table pressing against hers. "I got a room at the Peninsula. I know you always wanted to go there."

So this was how he did it. He just lied to whoever was home with the kids – his wife, say it, he lied to his wife – he had so much work, important meetings, life-saving activities vital to the national interest – and then he cozied up in some dim corner with his floozy – now she was the floozy – she checked her top – still there – and he seduced her with a romantic dinner and his various charms while the wife, in her checked apron and fluffy house slippers, obliviously washed his children, wiped the counter, and watched the clock, waiting for the familiar tap tap of his footsteps in the front hall. Could she do this to Shawna, knowing how it felt, knowing that every touch of flesh to flesh was a tack pressed into her heart? And at least as important, could she do it to herself, knowing what Alex's love had once meant to her? She pulled her hand away.

"Meredith, I'm sorry, that was stupid. I just miss you. That's all. But I shouldn't have pressured you, I know – it's important. I'm sorry."

"I think this is enough for tonight. I'm tired, I want to go home." Meredith sat up straight and crossed her arms over her chest. And she did want to go home. Suddenly the safety of her old bathrobe and a library book sounded very good to her.

"I'll get the check." Alex raised his hand to the waiter and gave him his credit card. "Meredith, we will talk, I promise. Do you want to do it now?"

"No. When we're not so tired. And drunk." She smiled weakly. "Thanks for a lovely dinner. And Alex – I miss you too."

He pulled out her chair, and they went to find the valet.

Winston Bigelow sat on a bench in Gillson Park and looked at the vast black lake. He couldn't sleep tonight, not after all the revelry at his house, the eager parents clucking proudly around their children and preening about colleges applied to and gotten into, goals pursued and achieved, the bumper stickers to be displayed on the back windows of their large family cars. For the most part, the children didn't even seem to have academic interests they wanted to pursue, they weren't curious or passionate, they were just hamsters on a wheel, fulfilling social expectations. He had been like that too once, but not now. He couldn't believe how vapid they all were, how pointless and empty it all seemed.

Noticing the bite of cold, Winston wrapped his Burberry scarf tightly around his neck, the two ends over his shoulders, for added protection. The cold wasn't all bad. Its nip on his face brightened his mind, it blew his thoughts clean. He heard the swish of the waves brushing the shore, and under the dim glow of the old-style street lights dotting the path behind him, he could glimpse the white fizz of a few close columns of water before the dune grass between the beach and the bench hid them from view. He thought of his life, so much striving for success at his law firm, and of all his client companies, ultimately people, fighting over large sums of money. He had devoted years of his life to helping corporations defend against assaults on their businesses. That was his job, he was good at it, and he had been proud of it. He had worked hard, he had applied his considerable intellect, and he had risen to become a major litigation partner in a prominent Chicago law firm. In addition, he had provided much material comfort, a beautiful home and freedom from financial cares, for himself and his family. He had absolutely nothing with which to reproach himself, he had been a superb provider and a completely faithful husband. Any of the parents at tonight's party would puff up with pride and delight if their sons or daughters achieved half of what he, in his life's work, had accomplished.

Winston shifted and tucked his gloved hands into his pockets. He considered his own family, his wife and his son. Despite her intellectual and imaginative limitations, Pam had been a good wife, loving to him and to their son. Ricky was a cipher. He had been an adorable toddler, flaxen-haired like his mother, and bouncing with the thrill of exploring a new world. Now he was a teenager, and everything seemed to bore him. He was always tired, he didn't seem to want to learn or leap around or beat his chest. Now, in his youth, when he should have been seizing life, embracing it, inhaling armfuls of it, he didn't even want to leave the house. Ricky was doomed to follow his mother's path of laziness and mediocrity. Winston just didn't have anything to offer someone like that. At best it was frustrating, and at worst, it made him angry. Pam would miss Winston when he left, he knew that, though it was probably just an adjustment to managing her life without his guidance. He didn't think Ricky would even notice that he was gone.

The lake was dark, inky, creepy really. Winston knew it was there, stretching out for miles beyond the visible waves, melting into the black sky, but he couldn't see it, it was all blindness ahead. He was almost sixty years old. It didn't seem possible. Where had his life gone? He remembered long summers when he was a child, kicking a stone and sweating for what seemed like centuries.   Now the years rolled by in minutes. He couldn't just sink into it, carried on a relentless conveyor belt – next stop Scottsdale, then a nursing home, then death, punctuated by Ricky's graduations and wedding, and a lifetime achievement award from the bar association, if he was lucky. He still had a fine brain and a healthy body, and maybe twenty or even thirty years of life ahead before he had to face the inevitable. And, despite the fact that he was an old man at his law firm and the rushing nature of his existence, that was a long time. That was a chance for a whole new life, with new meaning and new people and new experiences.   A Crystal Cruise with Pam to Machu Picchu just wasn't going to do it. He had to be brave and resolute, he had to seize hold of the reins of his life and veer off the highway onto a muddy trail into the forest. Leaving the North Shore, moving to Hyde Park alone and studying philosophy was not exactly like climbing a mountain in the wilderness and seeing God, but compared to what he was used to, this next chapter would be a revelation. He needed to understand as best he could what was true and what was good, and to do that he needed to renounce all that was petty and conventional.   He wanted to see beyond this Wilmette bench, beyond the waves, into the meaning of the darkness.

　　　　He was awfully cold, he realized. He should get back home. Besides, he was starting to hear a few faint, possibly human sounds. He didn't know what time it was, he had lost track. Maybe the kids were starting to arrive after their long night of partying, though he doubted that, the sky still looked black. The waves washed up and back, making their crackling, swishing sound, rhythmic and soothing. He hated to go home to the mess, to beer bottles and Pam's fretting and Ricky's cold shoulder. He would just sit for a few more minutes, he thought, settling back and closing his eyes.

The footsteps were so quiet, almost inaudible, and his mind must have been somewhere else, maybe half asleep, maybe skittering around the cosmos or the edges of his own unconscious. He felt a pressure on his shoulders, and for a split second he thought that it was Pam, come to massage them after a hard day's work. And then he heard a voice say, "Goodbye," a familiar voice, and he felt an awful tightness around his throat. His hands pulled from his pockets and grabbed instinctively for his scarf, trying to loosen it, as his boots grappled ineffectually against the icy, sandy ground. He tried to speak, to cry out, to turn about and see the person behind him, but it was too late. All he could do was face the black abyss before him and clutch and gasp, until, finally, he stopped fighting, and the hands gripping the scarf, his own, released, and his killer slipped off into the cold night.

Chapter Nine

Nicole shifted restlessly in bed. Propping herself halfway, she tugged a decorative pillow from the floor and stacked it on top of her squashed flannel one. She had been flipping back and forth for hours, taking a pillow out, putting it back, in a vain attempt to trick herself into oblivion. But the bed was so hot, the damn flannel sheets, even without Michael steaming it up and flopping his hand onto her belly. Michael was a sweat machine. He would lie damply, faintly snoring, and when he turned, hot air would puff onto her like a bellows. Sometimes he would reach over and lay a hand on her leg in a semi-conscious, companionable way, and all the heat from his body would concentrate there, increasing her discomfort. Michael could always sleep, whether he had stress at work or she was in labor or Kelsey was out on a sketchy date. He would profess anxiety and then drop off immediately and effortlessly. Nicole, on the other side, frequently struggled, especially between 2:00 and 5:00 a.m., covers on, covers off, side to back to side. Maybe Michael slept the sleep of the innocent, and she had a guilty conscience.

Well, Michael wasn't here tonight, she could revel in her freedom. Nicole flipped on the lamp and picked up a novel from her bedside table. She was reading *Crime and Punishment*, that classic of guilty consciences. Now that the axe murder was over and Raskolnikov was in his own head all the time and vaguely considering Christian conversion, the book was a lot less interesting, and she couldn't focus. Where was Michael, anyway, this was his second night gone. It wasn't fair for him to worry her like this, and it wasn't fair to the girls. She of course had known that he wouldn't be pleased to find out that she had slept with Winston and that she had omitted that detail in her earlier confession, but she had come clean as soon as she knew that Winston was leaving the firm. Someone in this family had to work, after all, and Michael would certainly have quit his job if he had known about Winston earlier -- the past two nights constituted Exhibit A. She had permitted Michael to adjust in stages – first to the infidelity, and second, that accomplished, to the Winston aspect.

Thank god Michael had skipped the party at the Bigelows' house. He was understandably upset when he slammed out Friday night after her revelation, and his hauling off and socking a leading partner, even a lame duck, in the face and in his own home, would probably not have played well at work or with the other New Trier parents. And the last thing she needed was the whole North Shore and all of Winters & Early buzzing about why her husband had knocked Winston cold. Well, Winston had torn down their old house and built his heinous mansion, maybe they could have foisted it off on that. That's probably what Winston himself would have ascribed it to, Nicole thought, for she had chatted with Winston at the party, and he seemed to be his usual charming, oblivious self. Either he didn't remember their Polynesian rendezvous due to the large number of rum-based beverages he had consumed there, or he considered the incident to have occurred so long ago and to be so insignificant that he had completely jettisoned it from his consciousness. Winston lived intentionally – maybe he couldn't cope with the thought that, in an impulsive drunken moment, he had violated his own code of conduct, and he had buried that inconsistency so deep that even Dr. Freud couldn't unearth it. At the party, Winston even told her that he thought she should return to Winters to take his place, because he considered her "a fine legal mind and a model of moral rectitude." That had shocked her. She didn't know whether to be insulted or relieved. Then his wife broke some glasses, and she found herself talking to someone else.

The phone rang, loud and shrill. Nicole checked the clock – 5:30 a.m. The twins must want a ride home. Though the sun hadn't yet emerged, they must be tired after an entire night of prancing around in trash bags. She would take their dates home too, if need be, that was her job on Turnabout night. Normally, gallant Michael would have volunteered, but at the moment, she was the only parent in evidence.

"Hello," she said calmly into the receiver while swinging her legs out of bed.

"Mom, it's Abby."

"Yeah, Honey, do you guys need a ride? Where are you?" Nicole stood up and groped with her toes for her slippers.

"Umm, yeah, but it's worse than that. Could you just come to the beach – right now?"

"What's wrong, Honey? Are you all right? Is Kelsey okay?"

"Yeah, we're fine. The police are here now. Actually, we, umm, found a body. Mom, please come now. I'll tell you more when you get here. Is Dad home? Bring Dad."

"I'll be right there, Abby. Don't move."

"Okay."

"See you in a minute."

Nicole yanked random pants and a sweater out of her dresser and threw them on. A body at Gillson beach. That was too bad, and traumatic for the kids. Every once in a while, some poor soul fell off a boat and washed up on the shore there. But it was winter, definitely a weird time for a sailing accident. Maybe someone screwing around on the stone pier and fell in, and with the water so cold, they wouldn't last long. How horrible.

She hoped it wasn't a New Trier kid who had gotten drunk and done something stupid.

Rushing toward the front closet, Nicole ran down the stairs into the living room. She stopped in surprise. Michael was flopped on the couch, and even with the noise of the phone and her rummaging and clomping, he seemed to be asleep. Despite her concern for the girls, her mood lifted. Michael was home. He loved her, he couldn't stay mad at her for long. She reached out and touched his hand. He was freezing. She ran to the closet and grabbed her down jacket and his overcoat. Tucking the coat tightly around him, Nicole paused for a moment to stroke his hair and to listen with relief to his regular breathing. Then she threw on her jacket, grabbed her purse, and hurried out the back door. Thank goodness, Michael was home. He loved her, he would forgive her. Things would get better from here.

The sky over the lake had barely started to lighten to a grim, faded gray. Abby, in her winter coat, stood on the grass in front of the blinking police car blocking access to the lane beside the beach. Behind her, technicians loaded an inert body into an ambulance flanked by multiple police cars containing shivering teens, waiting for their parents.

"So, umm, how's it going, Abs?"

Abby's date Freddy shifted from foot to foot. Despite an early show of chivalry, when he scotch taped a corsage to her trash bag and scooted in next to her on the minibus, Freddy had soon decided that he would have more fun propping up a tipsy Renee Van Streusel, who, Abby later learned, had asked another guy to the dance in a successful ploy to make Freddy jealous. Abby was just an invisible cog in the wheel of the Van Streusel man-eating machine, not much of a change from her usual role in New Trier social life. Still, this being her only date in her entire high school career, it was depressing. And just when she had thought it couldn't get any worse, what with Freddy holding Renee's bare shoulders at the afterparty while she puked, and Kelsey in a dark corner of Ricky Bigelow's basement making out with Brandon, they had tromped over to the beach and found a dead body. The girls all started screaming and saying they were going to faint, and the boys looked a little green, between the beer and the corpse. So, of course she was the only one with sense enough to walk a few feet to the Coast Guard station and to call the police. This definitely was not her dream date.

"Freddy, I'm fine, I'm just waiting for my mom. Do you need a ride?"

"No, I'm good, my dad's on his way. Umm, thanks for a nice evening." He looked sheepishly at the snow-prickled grass, stomped flat by so many feet.

"Sure. Thanks for coming," Abby replied automatically. "Oh, here's my mom. See ya." She waved a gloved hand at Nicole, who had parked her car on the side of the road and was running toward her daughter.

"My gosh, what a thing!" Nicole exclaimed, giving Abby a hug. "Are you okay? Where's Kelsey?"

"Yeah, I'm fine. Kelsey's just keeping warm in a police car. Did you bring Dad? Where's Dad?" Now that her mother was here, Abby started to shake.

"Dad's at home. I didn't want to wake him up."

"Oh, that's okay, then," said Abby. What with the cold and the fatigue and the trauma, Abby's brain was starting to freeze. Her father was home. That, at least, was a relief. "Let's get Kelsey, I want to go home." She wouldn't say anything more to her mother right now, she didn't want to complicate things. She just wanted to get out of here.

Abby and Nicole wound their way between emergency vehicles and clumps of parents and children and police. They found Kelsey, Brandon's arm tightly around her, shivering against a car door. The flashing red and blue lights and the dim glow of the old-fashioned street lamps, with the dune grass and the bare trees and the choppy gray-green water, gave the place an unearthly aura, like a movie set in a sci-fi movie. Looking out over the lake, Abby half expected to see metallic paper plates whirling over the horizon toward the park lawn. Instead, pink and fuchsia streaked the eastern sky. Sunrise. It was beautiful, and it happened every day.

"Kelsey, are you okay?" Nicole grabbed Kelsey's free arm and rubbed it. At least Kelsey was now wearing a sweatshirt and jeans, but she had to be freezing. "Brandon, do you need a ride home?"

"Yes, thanks."

Nicole touched the shoulder of a passing policeman. "Excuse me, is it all right if I take these kids home?"

"Do we have your names and information?"

They nodded their heads.

"So," said Nicole, staying with the policeman for an extra moment, "what happened? You always worry about your children with these awful late parties – it wasn't some poor kid, fallen in the lake, was it?"

"No, not at all. Adult male. We're waiting for his identity to be confirmed. And no water involved. I can't really say any more right now. You can take them home," the officer said, inclining his head toward her group, "but we'll be in touch."

"Why would you be in touch?" she asked.

"Well, I don't know for sure, but I guess you'll find out soon enough – this appears to be a homicide."

"Who is it?" Nicole asked.

Kelsey looked at her mother and grabbed Abby's hand. "Mom, it's terrible – we think it's Mr. Bigelow."

Abby watched as her mother's face went from red to white to petrified. She grabbed her heart and then her stomach. "I need to sit down." Nicole stumbled toward a bench facing the water.

94

"You can't sit there, Ma'am. See the yellow tape? Crime scene."

"Crime scene? The bench?"

"Here, you don't look so good. I'm finished for now – you shouldn't be driving, let me drive you all home. Now, what's your name again?" the officer asked. "Here, you can sit up front with me. How do you know Mr. Bigelow?"

"I'm Nicole Fisher, and we live on Gregory, west of Green Bay Road," she said, gathering herself. "These are my daughters. I'm a lawyer," she added. "And I think we'll just rest quietly now. We're awfully tired. Thank you for driving us home."

Meredith looked at the alarm clock beside her bed. It was only 6:00 a.m. on Sunday, her morning without the girls, but she couldn't sleep in. She would just have to consider this another opportunity lost to Alex's wandering eye. Because that's all last night's attempted seduction was about. Now that Alex had lost her, now that he had dumped her and married a child, and Meredith had adjusted, sort of, she was looking pretty great. Certainly it would be wonderful if he had finally realized – what? – that he had made a huge mistake, that he loved her, that he had always loved her. And, after a trip to the Peninsula involving a lot of thrashing and throwing down on the bed, they could all be a family again. That sounded like a fun romance novel, but not very realistic. If she and Alex did charge off on his white horse, leaving Shawna coughing up dust, would their marriage be any better than it was before? They were both intelligent people. Surely they had learned something in the last four years, and if they tried again, they would get it right. Maybe. Good intentions were no guarantee of good conduct, and Meredith wasn't even sure that Alex had those.

Meredith sat up out of her rumpled sheets and slid into her slippers. She padded downstairs, filled the coffeemaker, and peered out the living room window hopelessly. A blue plastic bag shone against the snow along her front path like a beacon of hope. It was a miracle, miracles happened! The newspaper was here early on a Sunday morning. She could drink her coffee, thumb through the *Tribune*, and turn off her brain. Maybe she would even make herself a couple of banana pancakes. Picking up the hem of her robe like a ball gown, Meredith stepped outside and slid along the front path. As she leaned over to grab the newspaper bag, a police car pulled up across the street and stopped. She stared as the back seat discharged Nicole, Abby, and Kelsey Fisher, all looking rumpled and exhausted. Meredith waved, and, as she started across the street, they turned and rushed up the walk to their front door. Luckily, she recognized the policeman, Brad Wood, an officer with a couple of years of experience, who had testified for her in traffic cases. He rolled down his window.

"Meredith, hey. Nice outfit. Very professional."

"You're out early, Brad. What's going on?"

"Looks like a homicide in Gillson Park. The victim was found on a bench, an apparent strangulation. An old guy, name of Winston Bigelow, though that's unofficial, we're waiting for the family to I.D. him."

"What do the Fishers have to do with it?"

"Girls found the body, along with some other New Trier kids. They went over to the beach after that Turnabout dance of theirs, and they got more than a romantic sunrise. I think a couple of the guys are heading over to the Bigelow house now, to talk with the wife and son. If you hurry, you might be able to get in on it."

"Thanks, Brad. I'll see what I can find out."

Meredith turned and scuffed along the icy walk. The newspaper would have to wait. She would make some calls and see if she could help out with the investigation. Wilmette was her home turf now, after all. And Maggie and Lucy were with their father and Shawna. Shawna wouldn't mind keeping them a few extra hours. She was always nice about that.

Chapter Ten

Her Honda popping along the quaint red brick of Michigan Avenue, Assistant State's Attorney Meredith Bennett drove determinedly toward the Bigelow house. Murder cases were rare on the North Shore, and almost always personal. Although the plights of those involved – the victims, their families, and sometimes even the killers – could be heartbreaking, this was the part of her job that was the most intellectually and emotionally challenging, and where she felt, ironically, the most alive herself. Her usual daily diet of petty crimes paid the bills and provided fairly regular hours for the care and feeding of her children, but that was a working mother's compromise. It was too bad, though, that somebody had to get killed to fling a little sparkle into Meredith's otherwise humdrum career.

On the east side of the quiet street, large houses sprawled between expansive front lawns and resort-like backyards sloping down to a wide sandy beach and the lake. Across the road, pleasant suburban brick and stucco houses stood closer to the curb and to each other, as they would on other Wilmette residential blocks.

While the west siders lugged their folding chairs down the sidewalk to join the riffraff on the public beach, their across-the-street neighbors simply opened their back doors and spilled out onto their own glorious slice of nature.   Meredith knew, however, from her possibly illegal but commonly accepted marches across the public beach and past the "Private Property" sign, that the unfenced private beaches were, for practical purposes, one enormous beach shared among all of the riparian neighbors. And although it was rare indeed for Meredith to stumble upon any of the owners out enjoying their bit of sand and water, she felt sure that tempers could flare if coke cans and inner tubes were left lying around to clutter up the scenery.   Oddly, these most successful private property owners were to some extent engaged in an experiment in communal living.   Owning a house on this street might be every Wilmette resident's dream, but Meredith could see how it could become a pressure cooker of status and resentment.

And then there was the teardown-McMansion problem.   Meredith passed a faded brick house on the lake side, a house likely built in the 1920's, with an attached one-car garage and a few tight, aging yews scantily skirting its ankles, to park in front of the Bigelow manor, a spanking new villa that was about as Italian as a pizza parlor in Disneyland. Its sleek stucco facade sported chiseled curlicues of scrolled marble around its numerous windows and imposing double doors.   The drive swept through an allee of miniature olive trees and a small grape arbor to pass between a fountain island and the front doors. Meredith knew that the longtime neighbors might resent new ones like this, for the imposition their noisy and dusty construction had caused, and for the implied disparagement of the old neighbors', well, old houses.

A police car sat across the street. Meredith walked up to it, and the officer stepped out.

"Hello, I'm Meredith Bennett, the prosecutor assigned to the Bigelow case. And you are…?"

He stuck out his hand. "Dan O'Brien."

"Has the victim been officially identified?" asked Meredith.

"Yes. Some of the parents at the scene did identify him as Winston Bigelow. A few of us came over here to inform the wife, Pamela Bigelow, of her husband's death, but she appears to have left the residence. According to the kids at the park, she also has a son, Ricky. He does not appear to be home either. I am waiting here in case either one of them returns to the residence, at which time I will call for additional support."

"Did any of you go into the house – I mean, it's possible that whoever killed Mr. Bigelow poses a danger to the rest of the family."

"That did occur to us, Ma'am, but we considered it unlikely and decided not to break into the residence. The kids reported that they were at a party at the Bigelows until about 4:15 a.m., at which time they walked over to the park. They discovered the deceased at about 4:30 a.m. When we returned to the residence, the house appeared to be undisturbed. There was no sign of forced entry."

"Well, it seems strange for no one to be home at, what is it," she checked her watch, "8:00 a.m. on a Sunday. It's possible that they're asleep after a very late night." Meredith considered whether she would want to be awakened after a few hours of sleep to learn that Alex had been strangled on a park bench and decided that, from Pamela Bigelow's point of view, it could probably keep a few more minutes. On the other hand, Mrs. Bigelow could be dead or injured in there. She also could be the killer. "Dan, why don't you call for back-up now. I think we should go into the house."

A second car arrived five minutes later, and two young officers, Stark and McBride, stepped out. Meredith and the three police officers marched down the front walk, rang the Bigelows' doorbell, and then waited in uncomfortable anticipation. Nothing happened.

"Maybe we should go around back," Dan offered.

"Wait a minute." Meredith turned the brass knob and the door opened.

The place was a palace. She felt like Dorothy leaving her black-and-white farmhouse and emerging in Munchkin Land. First, they entered a circular foyer, the floor a swirling checkerboard of black and white marble. To their right and left, twin gold-framed oval mirrors hung on curved walls above matching side tables displaying vases of white tulips and half-drunk beer bottles. Twenty feet above loomed an enormous chandelier undoubtedly purchased from the set of the Italian production of *The Phantom of the Opera*. Between the mirrors, an archway opened to pale wood floors polished to a gleam, then Roman columns framing a glass wall through which the lake, today mostly a gray chop against a turquoise horizon, flowed in a diagonal toward the shore.

"Mrs. Bigelow," Meredith called. "Ricky!"

No one answered. The four intruders fanned out to investigate the house. Everywhere were signs of last night's teenage party – empty chip bags, used glasses, torn trash bags, and dozens of beer bottles in various states of decline. From all appearances, no adult had supervised, and certainly no one had cleaned up afterwards. Meredith could not imagine turning a blind eye to an underage beer bash in her own home, nor could she have tolerated such a mess. Maybe mother and son had checked into the Orrington Hotel until the cleaning crew arrived on Monday.

While Stark and McBride trooped downstairs to inspect the lower level, no doubt the scene of even more sticky substances, Meredith and Dan went upstairs to check the bedroom area. In the master bedroom, the king-sized bed's ten throw pillows in various sizes and shades of ecru showed no signs of disturbance – neither Winston nor Pam, nor, fortunately, any randy and/or intoxicated high school students, had slept in the bed that night. No one who would leave tipped beer bottles on the plush living room rug would have taken the forty-five minutes required to reposition all these accessories. Meredith was staring flabbergasted at the biggest shower stall she had ever seen – honestly, a horse could have soaped up in there if it could have climbed the staircase – when Dan called her.

"Meredith, I think I found Ricky." Her stomach turned as she rushed down the hall.

Dan was standing in the doorway of a teenage boy's Garden of Eden – a giant TV against one red wall, a computer on a desk against a blue wall, and on the floor, a rug which appeared to be made from a dead unicorn. Atop a large, circular bed knocked off from Shaq's crib, a naked foot protruded from a chaos of comforters and shaggy throw pillows. Meredith approached cautiously, searching for a head.

"Ricky, are you in there?"

"Huh?" With relief, Meredith observed an explosion of covers, as a boy's greasy, confused face emerged from the center of the bed. "Mom?"

"No, Ricky. I'm Mrs. Bennett, and this is Officer O'Brien. We're looking for your mom. Do you have any idea where she is?" Meredith peered doubtfully at the sleepy boy, who smelled like a locker room after a Super Bowl victory.

"Isn't she here?"

He sat up, his lower half still modestly under a blanket. His Chicago Bulls tee shirt, washed to a thin softness, hung loosely like a smock. As Ricky scratched and blinked, trying to wake up, Meredith felt her heart tighten with concern for this fatherless child, just the fragile bud of a man.

Carefully, she perched on the edge of the bed. "Ricky, we need to talk to your mom, it's important. She isn't home. What happened here last night?"

"Umm, we had a party after Turnabout," he mumbled, so softly that Meredith had to strain to hear him.

"So, there were a lot of kids here?"

"Yeah. We didn't do anything wrong."

"No, I know, Honey. How long did they stay?"

"Well, the freshmen all got picked up pretty early. I don't know what time. Then I went to bed."

Meredith looked at Ricky. He had a smattering of small pimples on his nose, and a few wisps of dark hair on his upper lip. This had to be the worst age in the world – though maybe Maggie's was, twelve wasn't so hot either. In fact, skipping from ten to thirty would probably increase human happiness exponentially.

"Ricky, when was the last time you saw your mom and dad?" Meredith tried to make the question sound casual, but his eyes opened wide.

"I don't know. They were both here in the house somewhere, I guess. Yeah, they were letting the parents in." Ricky paused and considered. "Is everything okay?"

No, everything was definitely not okay. Ricky's father was dead, and his mother was, well, not exactly missing, but absent at an awfully early hour after a late night. Meredith considered telling Ricky about his father, but rejected the idea. They should tell Pamela first, and then she could break it to her son.

"Ricky, do you have any idea where your mother might be this morning? Does she have a job, or does she help out at church, anything like that?"

"She teaches yoga, but I don't think today. No church. Could you please go now?" He looked blearily at his covers.

"Sure, Honey, sorry to disturb you. I'm going to leave my card here, on your, um, bean bag chair. If your mom comes home, would you please have her call me?"

"Yeah."

As Meredith and Dan left the room, Ricky turned on his side and curled into a ball. Downstairs, they met Stark and McBride.

"It's a mess in the basement, and no sign of Mrs. Bigelow," said McBride. "We checked the garage – no cars. Oh yeah, that reminds me. I don't know if you heard -- a couple days ago, Thursday morning it was, Mrs. Bigelow's car was hit by a train. No one was hurt, she got out in time. Just got stuck on the tracks, I guess, and some kid helped her escape. Totalled her car. Kind of weird."

"Weird is right. Okay, thanks," said Meredith. "Maybe she left in her husband's car, then. Why don't you guys work your magic, try to find it. Something is going on with her." As they left, she pushed the side button to lock the front door. "I'm going to let the kid sleep. His world is going to crumble soon enough. Let's give him a few more minutes of peace."

Upstairs, Ricky scooted out of bed and shuffled to the window. Good, they were going. He knew more than he let on, a lot more than anyone thought. His father was leaving them, just moving out like they didn't even matter, like they were just so over he didn't even have to think about them anymore. His mom had cried for two straight nights, and Ricky couldn't stand that, and he knew it was his father's fault. Well, they didn't need that asshole. They were better off without him.

Ricky walked downstairs to get some juice. God, what a mess, kids were pigs. Well, he would pick up some of this stuff. That would make his mom feel better when she got home. He would show her that he could make her happy, that they would be fine without Winston. He got a trash bag from under the kitchen sink and began filling it with beer bottles. That was more than his dad would ever have done for her.

*

Meredith stood with the three cops in front of the Bigelow mansion. "Okay, we have a dead man, strangled with his scarf, and his wife is gone, and his son seems kind of out of it. I think Officer Wood has his hands full interviewing the kids who were at the crime scene. Let's talk to the neighbors, see what they know about the family, or if they saw anything strange last night. I'll go south, Dan, you go north, and you two guys slum it across the street. Let me know what you find out."

Meredith hurried next door, to a house that contrasted sharply with the Bigelows'. It was old, pink brick, a fine but faded house which the Bigelows would undoubtedly have torn down. She stopped in front of the painted white door and rang the bell. Excited toenails skittered across a bare floor, and sharp barking followed. As Meredith steeled herself for a dog attack, the door opened a crack.

"What is it?" A suspicious male voice siphoned outside.

"My name is Meredith Bennett. I'm from the State's Attorney's Office, and I wanted to ask you a few questions about your neighbors, the Bigelows."

"Finally! Come on in. Down, Angus."

The door opened to reveal a wiry, gray-haired man in plastic aviator glasses and an argyle sweater vest, tugging on the collar of a furry miniature Lassie. Easing herself through the door, she was disturbed to feel the dog's snout investigating her private parts in a very unprofessional manner. What was it with dogs and groins anyway? She pretended not to notice, as the seemingly triumphant man led her through his floral wall-papered foyer into his knickknack-ridden living room.

"Have a seat," he said, indicating a brown La-Z-Boy, positioned kitty corner to a matching brown La-Z-Boy, into which he now sank. They faced a picture window, framing a view of the lake. "Pretty, isn't it?" the man said, gesturing toward the water. "Well, not for long, if those Bigelows have their way. I'm glad you're finally taking my complaints seriously. Something has to be done, and I've taken it about as far as I can on my own."

"What's your name, Sir?" Meredith asked, removing a pad and pen from her purse and trying not to lean back, lest the lounge chair unfurl and leave her open to Angus's advances.

"Ned Haskell, that's who, I'm surprised you don't know. That Winston Bigelow is a menace, and I'm sure his wife is no better. Big shot lawyer, comes in here with all his money and clutters up the lakefront with his rubbish, ruining it for the rest of us. I've lived here for years, and I've never seen such selfishness. We've been trying to stop him from building his beach house, that's what," Ned said, responding to Meredith's quizzical look, "but we were having no luck, at least not until

108

today, when you showed up. And they were having a horrible, noisy party, last night, a bunch of teenagers with no clothes on, put that in your report too. I swear it was the last straw – Angus couldn't sleep for all the drunken orgies and blasting music – I suppose that's what they call it, anyway."

"Well, Mr. Haskell," Meredith quickly interjected, as Ned paused for his second wind. "That sounds terrible. So the neighbors are upset with Winston Bigelow?"

"Apoplectic, more like. We paid a lot of money to live on the lake, beautiful view, all that, and some of us have lived here for decades. Our own bit of heaven, that's what it is. Then along come the new people, throwing their money around like a bunch of kings, with their boats and their beach houses and all sorts of junk, right at the water's edge. And we all have to look at it, and it is not a pretty sight, let me tell you. We asked Bigelow nicely not to build the damned thing, and then not so nicely, I'll admit it, but he doesn't listen to any of it. It makes you think, that's all I can say." Ned stopped speaking abruptly.

"Makes you think what, Sir?" Meredith asked, trying to appear absorbed as Angus sniffed her boots.

"That's all I can say," Ned said, shutting down.

"So, Mr. Haskell, you were awake late last night. Did you hear or see anything unusual, besides the partying?"

"No, nothing at all. Just tossed and turned, tossed and turned. What's this about, anyway?" Ned eyed her warily. "Did those kids finally burn the damned thing down, because that would be a true public service."

"I'm afraid, Mr. Haskell, that there was a suspicious death in the park last night. Your neighbor, Winston Bigelow, was killed. You say you were in bed?"

"Yes, I was," he said gruffly.

"Is there anyone who can confirm that? Mrs. Haskell?" Meredith asked.

"I'm afraid that poor Eileen has gone to her reward. I live alone, unless you count Angus. What, do you suspect me?" Ned stood up, and Angus, slobbering, leaped to attention.

"It's just routine, Mr. Haskell. We're talking to everyone in the area. Were you out this morning, walking the dog – did you happen to see Mrs. Bigelow leave the house?"

"I didn't see anything, leave me alone. I thought you were here to help me, and you tricked me, you got me to talk under false pretenses. Well, you can't use it against me – it's entrapment, I know my rights! Now I want you to leave." Angus started barking.

"I'm sorry to upset you, Mr. Haskell, but your cooperation is very important. If you think of anything, please call me." She set her card on an end table between a Colonial lamp and a pair of porcelain milk maids.

110

"You'd like that, wouldn't you? Don't let the door hit you on your way out. The nerve of some people," he muttered, as Meredith hurried out the front door.

Dan O'Brien was back in his patrol car. Meredith jumped into the passenger seat to avoid the cold. "How'd it go?" she asked.

"Interesting," said Dan. "Apparently there was not a lot of love between Winston Bigelow and his neighbors. Did you hear about the beach house?"

"Indeed," she said.

"Of course the neighbors on the lake side of the street are the ones who are angry – especially the old neighbors, who don't like to see things change. But according to the witness I interviewed, Mrs. Goldblatt next door, the neighbor to the south side, Ned Haskell, was the angriest of anyone. She also said that, when the Village failed to respond adequately to their complaints, some of the neighbors figured that they were on their own and decided to start a Neighborhood Watch. In the winter they're only doing Saturday nights. She gave me the schedule for February. Guess who was supposed to be out patrolling last night? Ned Haskell."

Chapter Eleven

Winston had gone for a walk in the park in the middle of the night and left her with a house full of New Trier seniors whom she didn't know and certainly was not planning to babysit. When the freshmen had left around 1:00 a.m., Pam and Winston had said goodbye like proper North Shore parents who loved hosting teenagers mucking up their home and playing bad music, when they could have been asleep, unconscious, which sounded to Pam like the answer to everything. With twenty kids still in the basement doing God knows what, Winston had announced his walk. That was her husband alright. He was always delivering scheduling information. "I will be in Tokyo next week," or "I have a client dinner on Tuesday," or, "I am leaving you, have a nice life." There was no discussion, he expected her to adjust. So, he had decided to leave in the middle of the party. As usual, she was supposed to hold the fort.

Well, if Winston could abandon the house in the middle of the night to take a walk, so could she. Pam had pulled on her cashmere coat and her boots and a snug matching hat and scarf set, and then marched out of the double front doors. Damn, it was freezing outside! She stomped determinedly down the sidewalk toward Gillson Park. The street lights shone fuzzily, faintly illuminating bare trees and the hedges surrounding dark front lawns. She picked up her pace, as if the swift click-click of her high-heeled boots on the pavement would somehow protect her from murderers and rapists lurking in the bushes. From the southern edge of the park, she could see the Bahai Temple, a huge dome of lacy white concrete, lit and shimmering several blocks away. Maybe that should have given her hope. It was the light of everyone's God, glowing with love and justice. How, then, to explain her crappy life, how to explain the existence of Winston, who could recreate himself and thrive, like some mutating, flesh-eating virus? Oh sure, it was all beyond human understanding, that was the answer. Some answer. Either that or it was all a big lie, like her life.

Pam had walked down the lane toward the lake and the benches. It was so dark, and she felt so alone. And then she saw him, his back relaxed on a park bench, so quiet, so peaceful, thinking his own thoughts, when she had to race along as fast as she could just to keep warm. She stopped, watching him. Could he feel her behind him? They were married, they should have a connection, and she could feel herself bristling, shooting long barbed wires of energy that should have pierced his back and arms and neck and head and caused him to turn and look at her. She could feel these darts and rays bursting out of her, thousands of them, pricking him, stabbing him. But Winston just sat there, deep in his own thoughts. Why couldn't he feel her, why couldn't she reel him in like a fish? If she were an axe murderer, she could raise her weapon in the frozen air and split Winston's skull like a pumpkin. Did he deserve it? He might. Would it help her? She didn't know. But she didn't have an axe. Killing Winston would require an improvised weapon. She could adjust, Winston had taught her that. He placed her in situations, and she was supposed to make due.

Twenty minutes later, Pam found herself back home. She must have walked on automatic. It was so cold outside, and her brain wasn't working properly. She had forgotten her key. It was a good thing the partiers were here, she hadn't even locked the front door. Pam grabbed her purse and headed for the garage. She was tired and confused, and she needed to get out of here, she needed to run, and she needed to sleep. Double damn, she had forgotten, the train, her Lexus was a tangled mess at the auto body shop. Rushing back into the house, she plucked Winston's Mercedes keys from the basket on the kitchen counter. Too bad, Winston. He wouldn't have the chance to scold her about this.

Pam drove around for a while, a long while it must have been, though she had lost all sense of time. She drove north to Lake Forest, where the iron gates of icy mansions punctuated wintry Sheridan Road like hyphens on a blank page. Then she turned the Mercedes

114

south and drove all the many miles through the North Shore to Lake Shore Drive, the ever-present lake sloshing angrily toward her from across eight lanes of traffic. She slipped off the Drive into downtown Chicago, near the fancy hotels – the Ritz, the Four Seasons, the Park Hyatt – and suddenly she was so tired, she could hardly stay awake. The sheets in those hotels – Winston used to treat her for anniversaries, with special Saturday night stays there, and even though she knew he got a corporate rate, it was romantic. The sheets felt so crisp and smooth, and sometimes she took a bath, a hot, perfumed soak, which, even though she had a Jacuzzi in her own house, was just so much better at the Ritz. She could go there now and sleep, she felt like she could sleep forever. Wouldn't that be wonderful, just to sleep forever.

Pam slid the Mercedes up to the Ritz entrance, and a doorman in a fur hat leaped from his station under heat lamps by the front doors. "Checking in, Madam?" he asked, and Pam remembered going to London with Winston on their honeymoon, to the Dorchester Hotel, where everyone had called her Madam, and she had been so thrilled because yes, she was married, and it felt so strange, how did they all know?

"Yes, checking in," she announced, and the doorman gave her a valet ticket and said a few things she didn't hear. "No bags," she said, and she paused. "The name is Bigelow. I'm meeting my husband," she announced.

"Certainly, Madam," the man said, bouncing his fur hat. Yes, that had been the right answer. A second bellman held the door for her, and she swept in and up the elevator to the lobby.

The lobby was beautiful. Had it always been so lovely, with a large fountain in its center and so many flowers, orchids and nauseatingly sweet-smelling lilies and bowls of water floating gardenias so perfect they looked like porcelain. But it all seemed hazy, like a cloud before her eyes, like a dream or a vision. This must be what heaven is like, she thought. I have come to the right place.

Somehow she negotiated the check-in. She pulled out an American Express card and signed a paper and yes, if a suite was all that was available first thing in the morning, she was delighted to have a suite, that was what she wanted anyway. No, no luggage, her husband would arrive later with all of that, it was a birthday surprise! His name was Winston Bigelow, and this was heaven, and soon they would be together.

After interviewing Ned Haskell next door to the Bigelows' house, Meredith decided to return home for lunch. As her car clunked west, the houses became more modest until, literally crossing the train tracks, she reached her own wooden split-level on Gregory in west Wilmette. She had moved from a similar house in

Skokie, though the Wilmette one did have an "updated kitchen" – realtor-speak for, "don't expect a Subzero refrigerator, but you won't have to wince at an avocado stove either" – and the Skokie shag carpeting had resumed its former position as somebody else's nightmare. The Wilmette house was small, but it had a bedroom for everyone, and it was in a dream school system closer to Alex. Closer to Maggie's and Lucy's father – that was the point.

Meredith stuffed her keys into her coat pocket, walked into the kitchen, and pushed the button on the answering machine. "Meredith, it's Officer Brad Wood. We were inspecting the perimeter of the Bigelow house, and I had occasion to enter the backyard. There I observed the foundation of the beach house, which I believe several of the neighbors mentioned in their statements. Scrawled on the side facing the main house were the words 'Yankee Go Home,' in what appeared to be black paint. Mrs. Bigelow has not returned to the residence." Beep beep.

Yankee Go Home, huh. Meredith poked in the refrigerator for a bowl of leftover spaghetti, flung it in the microwave, and stuck a teabag in a mug of water, to wait its turn to be zapped. Although defacing property had teenaged vandal written all over it, she hardly thought that a New Trier student, sophisticated in the ways of cool and oblivious to enemy mottos from, she guessed, the last World War, would have come up with that particular invective. That sounded more like an old geezer, say, Ned Haskell – which might explain his fib about staying home last night. Meredith had a hard time imagining Ned yanking brutally on the ends of Winston's scarf, and she wasn't sure that he was strong enough to do the deed and stay upright. Maybe if Angus tugged one way and Ned the other – even a bite-sized Lassie might be a clever and helpful dog.

She sat down with her lunch and stirred the pasta, to distribute the heat. Well, she would probably have to talk with Ned again later, but for now she would let him stew. With Dan O'Brien camped out in front of his house, Ned wasn't likely to make a getaway. And stew he would, he had been so angry. Guilty conscience? Or was he just a cranky old man?

Meredith pondered as she licked sauce off her lips. Luckily she enjoyed leftovers, since she always cooked enough food for four people. Would Dr. Freud suggest that, unable to accept her husband's absence, she was still making his dinner every night? Truth to tell, when Alex had lived with them, she had always cooked enough dinner for five people. She just wanted to make sure everyone got enough to eat. Surely that was all it was.

And yet, it was an interesting question. How much was her unconscious in charge? She was an intelligent, independent woman, and she felt that she was in control, making deliberate choices in her life. Sometimes people were victims of circumstance or chance or of other people's choices. But maybe we were all, in some way, also victims of our own secret wishes and secret guilt. Maybe we were our own worst enemies, and we didn't even know it.

Several minutes later, Meredith tucked her rinsed bowl into the dishwasher, threw on her jacket, and crossed the street to the Fisher house. As partners at Winters & Early, Nicole and Michael might be able to flesh out a portrait of Winston Bigelow's work life. Meredith also wanted to chat up Abby and Kelsey, since they were in the group that found the body. She rang the doorbell and waited. Nicole opened the inner wooden door, but she left the screen door closed.

"Hi, Meredith. I thought it might be Officer What's-His-Name. He said he would bring my car back. Do you know anything about that?" Through the screen mesh, Nicole's face looked puffy and pink, as if she had been crying.

"Nicole, I'm sorry to disturb you. This must be a difficult time. Winston Bigelow was one of your partners, wasn't he?"

"Yes, that's it. And the girls, finding him – I mean, with a lot of others, of course – the whole thing's hard."

"Well, I was concerned about you, but I was also wondering if I could talk with Abby and Kelsey for a minute. I'm assigned to the case, and I wanted to ask them what they saw."

"Really, this is not a good time. They already talked to the police, and they're exhausted. They're sleeping right now."

"Mom, are we out of Diet Coke again?" A whine came from the back of the house. Meredith looked pointedly at Nicole.

"Oh, okay, come on in," she sighed, sweeping her arm open in annoyed surrender.

Meredith hurried up several stairs to the living room and continued into the kitchen. Slathering mustard on a slice of wheat bread, Abby stood barefoot in plaid pajama pants and an old tee shirt. A spray of curly brown hair sprouted from a scrunchy on top of her head like an anemone. In the opposite corner, Kelsey's butt stuck out from the open refrigerator as she flipped past plastic containers searching for a can of pop.

"Hi, Mrs. Bennett," said Abby. "How are Maggie and Lucy?"

"They're fine, thanks." Meredith hoped they were fine anyway, but she wasn't too interested in them at the moment.

"Kelsey, close the fridge. If there's no soda, you'll have to drink water." Nicole was close on Meredith's heels.

"Water. Yuck." She scooted herself backwards onto the counter and perched. In pink terry cloth shorts and a shrunken tee shirt, Kelsey looked like she needed a square meal. Mourning her zero calorie soft drink, she swung her bare legs in a hypnotic, rhythmic motion.

"So," said Meredith, "I know that you two were in the group that discovered Mr. Bigelow in the park this morning. Did you notice anything else unusual while you were there?" Meredith flashed her glance between the two girls.

"Nope," Kelsey said immediately, swiveling her legs and adding a blonde hair flip. "A dead body was weird enough."

Abby thought for a moment. "I checked the ground, for footprints, you know, since there's still some old snow. But it all looked really trampled around the bench, I couldn't tell anything from that. I thought it was strange that whoever it was, the murderer, had tied the scarf onto the bench, had poked the ends through the slats and tied a knot. I guess that kept Mr. Bigelow from standing up and turning around to face the killer, but do you think that would help somebody weaker do it – I mean, they wouldn't have to hang on as long, and he might just choke himself while he struggled."

"Abby!" cried Kelsey, at the same time that Nicole said, "Abby, that's enough," and they both looked queasy.

"Also, that means the killer was behind him, so he wouldn't have to look at his face while he died. Maybe that means it was someone close to the victim – or maybe it was just easier that way," Abby added. She seemed to be done.

Meredith stared. "I didn't know that Mr. Bigelow was tied to the bench by his scarf. Did the police find him that way?"

"Well, no. Kelsey's boyfriend Brandon untied him. It took a while, the scarf was pulled so tight, and the wool had no give, and Brandon was panicking. But we couldn't just leave him like that, maybe he was still alive. But he slumped over on the bench, and we knew then that he was dead, so we left him like that."

"Did anybody tell the police all this?" Meredith asked.

"I don't know, I don't think so." Abby looked at the floor, then glanced up guiltily. "We knew we shouldn't touch anything, and we didn't want to get in trouble, but Brandon just did it."

"And you are telling me now, because you decided you should tell the truth?"

"Yes." Abby tilted up her chin. "And because I think it might affect your theory of the case, of who did it, I mean. Because it wouldn't have to be, for example, a grown man. It could be just about anybody."

"It was probably just some mugger or some psycho. I really doubt it was anyone who knew him," Kelsey said firmly, as if that resolved the issue.

They all turned toward a shuffling on the stairs. Michael came into the room scratching his armpit like a gorilla in the ape house. His dark hair stuck out on his head in random tufts. Meredith remembered seeing him bolt out of the house on Friday night. From the smell of him, he hadn't bathed since then, and from the look of him, most of his sleep had occurred in his clothes in an abandoned woodshed.

"Ah, my loving family," he pronounced in a sneering, unhinged sort of way. "And Meredith, perfect. To what do we owe this pleasure?"

Kelsey and Abby stared at their father as if he were a scary clown popping out of a jack-in-the-box. Nicole swiftly rose and grabbed a handful of his crumpled shirt. "Okay, Buddy, you're not ready for prime time. Why don't you go upstairs and take a nice, hot shower, and we'll talk later." She attempted to steer him towards the stairway, but he shook her off and planted his bare feet.

"No, no, I want to see my loving family, and you especially, Dear." He leered at Nicole.

Abby stepped toward her father, with Kelsey right behind her. "Come on, Dad," she said. "You're all tired out. You should rest."

"Don't try to boss me around, Young Lady!" Michael glared at Abby. "Are you turning into your mother on me? Well, I'm not surprised, though maybe little Kelsey here is a more accurate version. You should put on some pants, we have company. So, what's going on, anyway?" he asked, turning to Meredith. "I doubt this is just a friendly neighborhood visit. Did you bring a pie?"

"Actually, Michael, if you just woke up, you may not have heard about this. I came to talk with all of you about the death last night in Gillson Park." Michael pinched his lips together and waited. "Your daughters found the body, and I'm afraid you and Nicole know the victim."

"Then I suppose you are here in your official capacity. So, who's dead?" Michael straightened up and put on a solemn expression, as if he were now about to play a supporting role in a domestic tragedy.

"Daddy, I think you and Mom should go upstairs, so she can tell you in private. We all know how totally much you loved Mr. Bigelow…oops." Kelsey blanched. Well, no one in this house had slept much last night.

"Winston is dead," Michael said slowly. Nicole could not take her eyes off him. "What happened?"

"He was sitting on a bench in the park in the middle of the night, and someone strangled him with a scarf. I'm sorry," said Meredith. "I'm sure this is a shock. I was hoping that you and Nicole could give me a picture of Mr. Bigelow, and of his wife too, if you know her."

"How is, umm, his wife doing?" Michael asked, as he beckoned Meredith into the living room. Nicole followed, and she gestured for the girls to stay back.

"Actually, we don't know. We haven't been able to find her yet." Meredith settled into a cushioned blue chair across from the couch, where Michael lounged and his wife perched stiffly.

"Well, that seems fishy," Michael said. "She put up with a lot from Winston. Maybe she finally just snapped."

"What do you mean?" Meredith asked.

"Winston was leaving the firm to get a PhD in philosophy," Nicole interjected. "Maybe she didn't like that. They have a fancy house, an expensive lifestyle – maybe she was afraid that would end."

"Yeah, and if she killed Winston, she could collect his life insurance and stay on the gravy train. Still," Michael wrinkled his forehead thoughtfully, "it seems awfully calculating for a North Shore housewife. Though she was married to Winston – he might have taught her a thing or two about betrayal."

"What do you mean?" Meredith asked.

"He was a tough litigator," Nicole said quickly. "Sometimes they have to be crafty. As I'm sure you know, Meredith," Nicole said, smiling conspiratorially.

"I tend to agree with Michael, it seems like there would have to be more than Winston quitting his job," Meredith said, ignoring the last. "Have you heard anything about their marriage? Any affairs, indiscretions, anything like that?"

Nicole squeezed Michael's leg. "Nothing," she said. "He may have had some business enemies. He was a big-deal litigator. The job can get nasty."

"Nasty enough to kill him?"

"Well, probably not," Nicole admitted.

Michael turned to his wife. "Dear, why don't you get Meredith something to drink. I'm sure she would like a cup of tea on a cold day like this, and with so much work to do. Wouldn't you, Meredith?"

"That sounds wonderful. Thank you." Apparently Michael-the-slightly-unhinged wanted to tell her something in private. She hoped he hadn't hidden a handgun under a throw pillow.

Reluctantly, Nicole walked into the kitchen. Michael leaned forward confidentially. "So, I suppose I should tell you something. Draw the sting, as we say in the business." Meredith waited. She could hear water running. "After Nicole left the firm, we sold our house to Winston. He tore it down and built his fabulous Tuscan villa. I think Nicole resented it a little. But not enough to kill him, of course." He smiled. "At least, I don't think so."

"Why did Nicole leave the firm?" Meredith asked.

"An excellent question," Michael replied. "I suppose you will have to ask her that one."

"Michael, this is strictly routine – where were you last night between the hours of 1:00 and 5:00 a.m.?"

"Ah, Meredith, you sound so professional. Well, I was sleeping here in bed with my lovely wife, wasn't I, Dear?" he asked, as Nicole hurried into the room with a mug of lukewarm tea.

"Yes, of course," she said, setting the cup on a coaster next to Meredith. "Where else would he be?"

126

Meredith examined Michael's scraggly appearance doubtfully. "Some parents wait up for their children when they go out at night. Not you two?"

"Oh, no," Nicole said, smiling brightly. "Our girls are seniors. We're over that."

Meredith nodded. "So, Nicole, Michael suggested that I ask you why you left the law firm."

"He did?" Nicole looked astonished.

"Yes," Meredith replied. "Why did you?"

"I'm sorry, but I don't see the relevance of your question," Nicole responded.

At least she didn't lie. So, this was a sore spot. She stood up.

"Michael, Nicole, thank you for your time." Meredith stuck out her hand, but no one took it. "Say goodbye to the girls for me. I'm sorry all of this happened, and I'm afraid I may need to talk with you again, as the investigation proceeds. I feel lucky to live so close to two people with some insight on the Bigelow family. That reminds me – did Kelsey and Abby know Ricky Bigelow?"

"Not really," said Nicole. "The picture party and the afterparty were at his house, but I don't think they were friends. He's a lot younger than they are."

"Makes sense," said Meredith. "Have a good afternoon."

As she walked out the door, Meredith was surprised to find Kelsey on the front walk. She must have thrown on a sweatshirt and sneakers and gone out the back door.

"Umm, Mrs. Bennett?"

"Yes, Kelsey."

"I know neither one of my parents would do anything like this, no matter what it looks like."

"Why do you say that, Honey?" Startled, Meredith looked at her with concern.

"They're like, good people. I mean, everybody makes mistakes, right? That's all I can say." Kelsey's eyes filled up, and she looked at her feet.

"Everybody does make mistakes," Meredith reassured her, and she put her hand on Kelsey's thin arm. "If you want to talk to me anymore, you know where I am."

Kelsey nodded and turned back toward the house, as Meredith watched her go. Yes, everybody makes mistakes, she thought. But something strange was going on in this house. Last year, Nicole had quit her job as a litigation partner at Winters & Early under mysterious circumstances. A few days ago, in an equally unusual move, Winston Bigelow had announced that he was quitting his job as a litigation partner at Winters & Early. Were these two events connected? What if Nicole had left because Winston had done something bad which related to her in some way – and then Winston, driven by guilt, had quit, in favor of the blameless study of moral virtue? But what would account for the passage of an entire year between the two departures? Did it just take that much time for Winston's guilt to grow, or for his unconscious to assert itself? And did his decision to leave the firm somehow trigger his murder?

Apparently, Kelsey and Abby thought that their parents might be implicated in Winston's murder, and that at least one of them had made a "mistake." Sometimes the trick in life was to figure out which mistakes called for forgiveness, and which ones called for revenge.

Chapter Twelve

Pushing her housekeeping cart three feet down the hall to Room 1612, Marta Calderon sighed and checked her watch. It was 4:00 p.m. Sunday, check-in time. By noon, she had cleaned all the rooms for guests staying another night on the sixteenth floor. Men in sports jackets and women in cashmere turtlenecks and chic leather boots had left for brunch and the Art Institute knowing they would return to clean sheets and fresh towels, their toiletries neatly arranged on a clean wash cloth, and a vee fold on the edge of their toilet paper. After noon, she had scrubbed and vacuumed the rooms for new guests. Old soaps and shampoos were tossed and replaced with new ones, laundered white terry robes were hung, one in the closet and one on the back of the bathroom door, and all waste baskets were emptied and wiped clean. Normally, Marta took a break now. In an hour, she would begin turndown service, a second, more cursory cleaning -- new towels, drapes closed, and the radio tuned to soothing ocean sounds.

But Room 1612 was different. The guest, a Mrs. Bigelow, had checked in early, around 8:00 a.m. She had requested English Breakfast tea and a basket of croissants shortly afterwards, but she had never called in-room dining to ask that they retrieve her dishes. Maybe she had gone to Bloomingdales and forgotten. At any rate, housekeeping had not attended to Mrs. Bigelow yet today, and it was Marta's job to ensure that her guests on the sixteenth floor did not have to wade through the day's debris while they enjoyed their rooms. Marta decided to check on Mrs. Bigelow before she took her break. She knocked on the door, and when no one responded, she used her master key and entered.

The bathroom was immediately to her right. Crumpled towels were strewn on the floor, and Mrs. Bigelow seemed to have enjoyed all of the toiletries without replacing the caps on any of them. Straightening up, Marta noted that, oddly, the woman had no cosmetics bag, no make-up or hair brush or jewelry – which was too bad, she liked seeing the different lipsticks and creams, although standing them up neatly did get tedious. Next, she stepped down the room hallway to check the clutter in the bedroom itself. She stopped and gasped.

A small blonde woman lay askew on the king-size bed. Her clothes were neatly folded on its corner, her petite body drowned in a fluffy hotel robe, cinched around her waist. Sweat dappled her yellowish face, sour vomit soaking into the pillow under her mouth. On the bedside table stood a water glass and a tipped bottle of Midol Menstrual Complete. Near her left foot lay a note, on Ritz stationary. "Dear Maid, Sorry about the mess.

You can have this." Next to the note coiled a pearl necklace. Finally, a guest with a little consideration. Marta put the note and the necklace in her apron pocket and called her supervisor.

After several stuffy hours of Sunday afternoon paperwork and laundry, Meredith decided to take a chilly walk to clear her head. The Fishers were behaving strangely. Michael seemed hostile, for no discernible reason – though he was tired, and he was a lawyer, two strikes against him in the hospitality department. But why, if he spent the night in bed with his wife, did he look so exhausted and smell so bad? And when Nicole had answered the door, she looked as if she had been crying. Maybe she was mourning Winston, who was, after all, her partner. But she didn't show any sorrow in front of her husband, who was also his partner, and who appeared to grieve Winston as much as he would a dead chipmunk in the garage. Well, Winston did tear down Michael's house, and there may have been some backbiting at the law firm.

Nicole's decision to quit her job was still a mystery, but it seemed unlikely that the circumstances of her departure over a year ago had anything to do with Winston's death. Kelsey and Abby were awfully jumpy, and Kelsey clearly was trying to shield her parents. Were the twins hiding something? The whole family seemed to be trying to solve the crime. Maybe that was just human nature. But both adult Fishers were eager to pin the death on Winston's wife, Pam, who was still missing in all of this.

As she had intended, Meredith had learned a little more about Winston from the Fisher visit. She had already known that he was a very successful partner, both professionally and financially. And he was leaving the firm to pursue a PhD in philosophy. Well, if that wasn't true, it certainly was a whopper. He could take a couple classes as a cover and then do what he really wanted to do – which was to ride around in a red convertible all day with a twenty-year-old Hooter's waitress for company? As a goal for a sixty-year-old rich guy, that would, sadly, be more believable, but Meredith didn't think he would have to quit the partnership for that. That sort of behavior would cause some excited chatter, but it was his personal life, and it might even be a feather in his cap in some business circles.

Meredith didn't want to think about it. She hoped that life meted out a punishment for hurtful decisions. The woman would be so young or dumb or craven that Winston would soon come to see the error of his ways and regret wounding the beautiful, appropriate – well, Pam must already be a lot younger than Winston with Ricky running around, but more appropriate anyway – family that he had betrayed for the last hurrah of his dwindling manhood. But Meredith really wasn't sure if this sort of justice did happen, at least more than occasionally. Shawna.

She turned the corner and walked more briskly. Winston might lie to the firm if there were something illegal or work-related about an illicit relationship. Maybe he was involved with some young female associate at work? Not great, but if she weren't complaining, that could still be okay. If she were accusing him of sexual harassment, he might well end up out of a job. In the Hollywood version, the associate might end up dead – but not Winston.

What if Winston were telling the truth? What if, approaching his sixtieth birthday, he had contemplated the temporary nature of his existence, examined his life, and decided that he wanted to devote his remaining years to seeking real meaning. He had plenty of money. He could stay with his family in Wilmette – yes, they might have to move to a more modest house, but that's not terrible, as Meredith could attest. He might be more of a jerk and want the family to move to Hyde Park near the university to accommodate his quest – staring at one's navel might not give you the vision to notice anyone else's navel, at least initially.

Alternatively, it was possible that he had decided to completely blow up his life, jettison the wife and kid, and go exclusively intellectual ascetic. Somebody might do that, and it might even be a legitimate choice. It's your life, you only get one, if you think it's time to try something else, maybe you should do it. Selfish, but

134

Meredith could see its validity too. But not in America in 1997, no one would believe it. Everyone would think that, ultimately, once you peeled back all the highfalutin frills, what you would find is a naked male body part standing at attention. And who would think that more than his wife, Pam? Who was still missing. Where was Pam? By now her absence had morphed from trip-to-the-Jewel to woman-on-the-run. And running was never a good look.

Meredith turned the corner again and saw a car that looked a lot like Alexander's. Approaching, she saw the Evanston Hospital parking sticker – yes, Alex's car for sure. He must have brought the kids home, very nice of him. She rounded the last corner, hurried up the walk, and opened her own front door.

"Mommy!" Lucy ran up and hugged Meredith's waist as if she had just returned from wintering in Outer Mongolia instead of weekending two miles away. The house smelled delicious, of broiling meat and garlic, with a hint of homemade bread.

"We're in here!" Alex called. She found him in the kitchen stirring a pot, his face flushed, while Maggie carried placemats to the dining room table. "I know you've been working today, and I thought I would save you the trouble of picking up the kids."

This must be what it was like to have a wife. It was utterly fabulous. In a discreet husbandly move, Meredith touched Alex lightly on his back. The cuffs of his blue button-down shirt were folded up to avoid splashes, and she resisted the urge to press the round, sparsely haired bump of wrist bone marking the start of his long, elegant hands.

"Thanks, this looks wonderful. Very thoughtful of you."

"Dinner will be ready in half an hour. I know it's early, but I thought for Sunday supper...." Alex met her eyes. They had always eaten early on Sunday when the girls were small. After a hot dog lunch, the four of them would pile into the car in all weathers for a family outing. Then home for naps, an early meal, and then, after dishes, a little conjugal one-on-one time – was that what he was thinking, after striking out last night? "I thought maybe we could have that talk later, while the girls are watching TV," Alex said.

"Talk about what?" Lucy asked, reaching up and stroking Meredith's hair. She did seem a little insecure. Or maybe she wanted something.

"Nothing, Sweetie," said Meredith, gently removing Lucy's damp paw. "Are you staying for dinner, then, Alex?"

"Wouldn't miss dinner with my best girls." Meredith opened her eyes wide. "Right, Mags and Lucy?"

"And we are baking homemade rolls," Lucy announced. "I popped the can. It was so cool."

"What about Shawna – won't she miss you?" Meredith asked Alex.

"Shawna is totally fine with it," Lucy proclaimed. "She knows that Daddy needs to spend time with his daughters, and she is not threatened by this. Also, she has Things of Her Own to Do."

"Really," Meredith said. So, Alex had told Shawna in front of Lucy that he was going to have dinner with his ex-family. Meredith very much doubted that Shawna was even remotely okay with this plan. But, at least Alex was honest about it. This time. That made a nice change for the ethical.

While Meredith changed into something more comfortable – corduroy pants and a pullover sweater, though, admittedly, she had tried on three sweaters before picking the one with the deepest v-neck – Alex completed his culinary magic and called her for dinner.

"This is nice," she couldn't help sighing, as she sat down to a steaming plate of sirloin steak, mashed potatoes, and the touted crescent rolls.

"We decided not to make vegetables, since no one really likes them," Lucy stated, bringing her mother up to speed.

"That's fine," said Meredith, and she and Alex smiled at each other. She had missed this, the conspiratorial amusement that only two parents can share when silently ridiculing their offspring.

"You're awfully quiet, Maggie," Meredith suddenly realized. "Is everything okay?"

"Fine," Maggie replied automatically, curling and uncurling her dinner roll.

"Did you have a nice weekend?"

"Yup, we did," said Lucy. "We had doughnuts, and we went shopping, and we saw a movie. It was rated R for language."

Meredith glanced at Lucy and then looked back at Maggie, who was now decorating her plate with her potatoes. "How's it going with Stacy?" Ideally, Meredith would have talked with Maggie privately, so she spoke in a hushed tone, simulating confidentiality.

Struggling between the preteen desire to freeze her mother out and the need to unburden herself, Maggie turned white and then burst into tears. "Mom, it's so terrible. I mean, I thought Stacy and I were friends. And every day she won't let me sit with her, and she is so mean, she is trying to be in the cool group and I am not cool. But she's the only friend I have, Mom, I don't have anyone else to sit with. Everyone has friends but me."

Oh my god, they never should have left Skokie, this is just what Meredith had feared. What kind of mother moves her daughter in seventh grade, when cliques are impenetrable, and the girls scratch each other with their sharp kitten claws. And of course the North Shore was exploding with Stacys, who thought only about their junior high social status and which leggings they were going to wear tomorrow. Kelsey Fisher had probably been a Stacy. Shawna flitted across her mind, but she buried her again.

"Well," Alex said thoughtfully, setting down his fork. "I know that you thought Stacy was your friend."

138

"But she was my friend, Dad, we did everything together, we had so much fun, I could count on her, Dad," Maggie inserted heatedly.

"She was your friend – then – I see that – but now – she has dumped you, she has hurt your feelings, she wants a different friend. Is that how a friend behaves?" asked Alex.

"No," said Maggie.

"Well, do you think you should keep going back to her then?" Alex asked.

"No," Maggie admitted. "But I still like her. And I don't know what else to do." She started to sniff. Somehow, this story sounded familiar. Meredith was riveted.

"I know it's hard, but I think you have to forget about Stacy. You have two choices. You can either find a new friend, or go it alone. Do you think you can do one of those things?" Alex looked at Maggie empathically.

"I can try," Maggie said, sitting up straighter.

"So, let's think about this," said Alex. "When you go to the cafeteria tomorrow, what are you going to do first?"

"First, I'll get my lunch."

"What is it?" asked Lucy.

"Alright, now you are carrying your tray," continued her father. "This is the hard part. You see Stacy, and she has an empty place next to her at the table. What are you going to do next?"

"I'm going to walk over to the peanut-free table and sit with Linda. There are always spaces there. Linda isn't very cool, and she's probably lonely. She would probably be happy if I sat down."

Meredith looked at Maggie, and then at Alex. This was amazing. She may have made a mistake marrying Alex, but allowing him to impregnate her was brilliant.

"Good," said Alex. "Oh, you don't have any peanuts, do you?"

"No. I bought lunch." Maggie smiled.

"Okay," said Meredith slowly, knowing she absolutely should not ask this, but needing to hear what Alex would say. "Suppose – I know this will probably not happen, but just suppose, that after all of this – maybe not tomorrow, but after some weeks or even months, when you are used to being apart from Stacy and have filled your life with other things – what if Stacy suddenly starts being nice to you again? Like, maybe being in the cool group didn't turn out to be such a barrel of fun after all, and she misses your old friendship? What should Maggie do then?"

Meredith turned and looked hard at Alex. His face reddened. He thought for a moment, staring at the butter dish. "I think Maggie would have to think long and hard before she let Stacy back into her life. Maybe Stacy learned something about the value of friendship. That's possible. But Maggie would have to be very careful before she trusted Stacy again."

"I'm bored," said Lucy. "What's for dessert?"

Meredith picked up her water glass. Alex could leave after dinner. She was tired. And they had already had their talk.

After Meredith finished the dishes, the telephone rang.

"It's Officer Dan O'Brien, Wilmette P.D."

"Yes, Dan, what's up?" Meredith cradled the phone on her neck and dried her hands on a dish towel.

"Well, I have an update. Our victim's wife, Mrs. Pamela Bigelow, has been admitted to Northwestern Memorial Hospital. She suffered an overdose of over-the-counter pharmaceuticals after an apparent suicide attempt in the Ritz Hotel in downtown Chicago. She is uncommunicative at this time due to her unconscious state, but the doctors believe that she will be available for questioning tomorrow morning."

Meredith sat in a kitchen chair and rubbed her forehead. "Thanks, Dan. Did she leave a note?"

"The Chicago P.D. processed the scene after they realized that Mrs. Bigelow was related to our local murder victim, but they did not find a note. A hotel maid discovered Mrs. Bigelow during a routine cleaning visit around 4:00 p.m. and called for help immediately. Mrs. Bigelow had checked into the hotel at about 8:00 a.m. this morning."

"So she could have been up in Wilmette at the time of the murder," said Meredith.

"As far as we know right now. We'll know more after we talk to her."

"I'll come to the hospital tomorrow morning. What about her son, Ricky? Has anyone checked on him?"

"Well, that's another thing. We tried to contact Ricky to tell him about his mother – we also wanted to tell him about his father, before he hears it somewhere else -- but we were not able to reach him either by phone or in person. Maybe he's at a friend's house." Dan sounded uncertain.

"So, now Ricky is missing," Meredith stated.

"If you want to put it that way. He may just be hiding out in the house. I rang the doorbell, but I did not go in and perform a search. Do you want me to go back, and to contact Social Services?"

"No, that's all right. He probably is with a friend, you're right."

There was no reason to think that Ricky was in danger, and the last thing the kid needed was to get picked up by Social Services. An informal care arrangement was certainly preferable at this point. Even if he were alone all day today, what harm could come to him? He was a big boy in a warm house with food in the refrigerator. The worst that could happen was that he would play too many video games and eat too many potato chips. He wouldn't read the paper or watch the news, kids didn't do that, so he wouldn't know about his father's death. Tomorrow was Monday, and Ricky would go to school. Surely the New Trier social worker would talk with him. Meredith would call the school tomorrow, after she talked with Pam Bigelow. The social worker would know how to handle this.

"Thanks, Dan. Let me know if anything changes. Otherwise, I'll be at the hospital tomorrow."

Chapter Thirteen

It was nine o'clock on Sunday night at the Bennett cottage-on-steroids in Kenilworth. Shawna sat alone, staring at gibberish on the television screen. Shifting a half-eaten bowl of ramen noodle soup from the coffee table onto a coaster, she guiltily rubbed at its ghostly circle on the table top, tossed a mauve throw pillow over it, and rested her pedicured feet there. Staring at her toes, polished a patrician peach, Shawna yawned and considered her life. Here she slouched, at the tender age of twenty-nine, alone on an ecru velvet loveseat with her appropriate toenails. Meanwhile, her neighbors had filed the leftovers from Sunday dinner in the Subzero, directed the au pair to tuck the kids in bed, and settled down for a snuggle in front of "Masterpiece Theater." A few years ago, the idea of a night like that would have made her fall out with boredom, but now it sounded – well, like less of a snooze than this.

A whiny squeal oozed through the gaps in the latticed living room windows. Damn, sitting home alone at night in this tomb of a neighborhood was creepy, and she did it, like, Every Night. And last night, lest she relax for a single moment, there was that murder in Gillson Park just a few short miles from here. And the police had not caught the murderer yet. He might be prowling around even now, but he wouldn't stay in the park, he was too clever for that. He would dive into a residential street and peep into the house of a solitary, defenseless woman, and then – well, that would certainly teach Alex a lesson about working at the hospital Every Night, but it would totally not be worth it because she would be raped or dead.

If Alex even were at the hospital. Because, let's see, he had taken Maggie and Lucy out for the afternoon, then he had popped home at, like, seven, and then he had grabbed his doctor stuff and left again. He had eaten dinner with the girls, that was cool, but Shawna totally did not trust their mother. Of course there was no way that old Meredith could seduce Alex, she was way past her sell-by date. The problem was The Kids. Shawna had not seen that one coming, that Alex would include his kids' mother in some kind of family-sized economy pack. Mostly that never happened in real life. Men hated their ex-wives, and they fought all the time about money. But Meredith was different. To put it bluntly, she was an adult or something. And while that should have been a turn-off, Alex seemed to like it more and more. Until Shawna actually wondered sometimes if Alex might prefer Meredith to her. Not her looks, of course. Just being with her.

A screeching noise came from – where – a tree in the wind? The joints in the house? The murderer scraping his butcher knife against the glass in the doors to the patio? Well, Shawna wasn't going to sit around here freaking out about getting slaughtered in the breakfast nook or about her husband playing house with his ex-wife. Which could not be happening, because Alex had picked Shawna over Meredith. She had to remember that. Given the choice, Alex had married her. But whatever Alex was up to, Shawna was not going to sit here another minute. She was beautiful, she was young, and she deserved to have some fun, not to be buried here in this expensive mausoleum decorated in colors she couldn't spell. One way or another, Alex was going to regret leaving her alone tonight.

Shawna tugged on her cowboy boots, shook out her blonde hair, and checked her teeth in the mirror. Slinging on her leather jacket and grabbing the back door knob, she hesitated. If the murderer were out there waiting to strangle her, she totally should not go outside. On the other hand, she wanted a margarita, some raucous music, and a man's eyes on her blouse buttons. Bracing herself, she turned the handle, dashed to the garage, leaped into her BMW, and locked the doors.

Okay, cool, she could totally run the murderer over now. But where to, James? She needed a down-market bar filled with thirty-something guys looking for company with a cute butt. She certainly was not going to find that in Kenilworth. And it was Sunday night, even the McDonald's in Winnetka had closed a couple hours ago. Rush Street in Chicago, though teeming with singles bars, was about forty minutes away, and she didn't know where to park. Well, there was an Irish pub across the street from the Holiday Inn in Evanston. If by some crazy stroke of luck it were still open, that just might work.

Shawna headed south down Sheridan Road. February in Chicago so sucked. No leaves on the trees, piles of dirty snow stacked at the corners of slick sidewalks, everything gray and white and frozen. Expecting a snarl of police cars or garish yellow tape, she slowed near the entrance to Gillson Park, but it looked quiet and normal. An alien landing his spaceship in the field wouldn't detect that an old man had been killed in there last night. An event so momentous, and poof, it had vanished, just like when you eat dinner in a restaurant, go to the bathroom, get your coat, and by the time you leave, your table has been bussed for the next customer. Shawna shivered. Well, Alex would miss her if she were gone. He might not know that right now, but she was about to teach him some appreciation.

She slid into a parking space in front of Tommy Nevin's Pub. Victory, the door opened! Warm air, the yeasty smell of spilled beer, and frantically blinking Christmas lights reeled her inside. She scanned the bar area, and then the wooden tables topped with plastic ketchup and mustard containers, for an ideal spot to order a drink. If the past were any indication, if she hadn't lost her edge after three years of sitting on her married duff in Kenilworth, all she had to do was perch somewhere, cross her legs, remove her jacket, and lean over. Her body pulled drunk men to her like a lasso. It was a gift.

Shawna selected a wooden stool by the bar. She dusted it with her scarf and then hoisted herself aboard, her breasts following seconds later. To her right, a group of young men, probably Northwestern students, drank beer and joked rowdily about something, it sounded like karma, though it might have been caramel. "What goes around comes around," a guy in a black tee shirt shouted over a very non-Irish recording of Led Zeppelin, and his pal in plaid flannel laughed raucously and sloshed his beer. To her left, a depressed looking forty-something in a corduroy sports coat stared at a basketball game on the suspended TV and compulsively consumed goldfish crackers. Tapping her foot ostentatiously, she waited for a fizzy cocktail magically to appear in front of her, but nothing happened. One of the students turned, banged his mug on the bar, and shouted, "Another round, barkeep!" This totally cracked them all up, for unknown, college-based reasons.

"Here, Honey, this one's on me." The bartender placed a foamy glass in front of Shawna. "Tough day?"

Shawna looked at the bartender, who smiled encouragingly. She had expected an impoverished grad student with unkempt but boyish black curls and dark circles under his eyes, but this dude looked like her dad. He was easily sixty, with a patchy gray crew cut, and a paunch under a worn Nevin's tee shirt. Suddenly Shawna relaxed, and she closed her eyes for a moment.

"I thought I might find some company here, but these guys...."

"Yeah. They wouldn't know what to do with a girl like you." One of the students chortled, elbowed Shawna in the back, murmured, "Sorry," into the air, and then resumed his conversation. "Or I could offer you a lonely business traveler." The bartender tilted his head toward the crackers guy, who was now robotically raising and lowering his mug. "Don't you have a boyfriend, a pretty girl like you?"

"A husband, actually." Shawna wiggled her left hand, and her giant diamond rings, which she had forgotten to remove before this lame escapade began, glittered in the mirrored light.

"Okay, so, where is he? I'm Joe, by the way."

Of course he was. "I'm Shawna," she said. "He's a doctor. He's at the hospital. He says." She looked down at the counter, and her blonde hair hid her face.

"Where else would he be, Honey? I'm sure he'd be with you if he could." Joe looked at her appreciatively.

"Yeah, you'd think, wouldn't you." Shawna met his eyes. "But he has a couple kids and an ex-wife, and I just have a bad feeling. I think she's trying to get him back." She tipped her chin forward, her hands in fists on the bar.

"That's crazy," said Joe, pouring another beer for Mr. Crackers. "You're sweet, you're a knockout, nobody could ask for more. And he picked you over her before – she already lost this one, Baby."

"I know it doesn't make any sense, but I feel like he's hiding something. And when they're together, when she's picking up the kids or something – they seem so – tight." Shawna flinched, remembering. How could Alex do this to her? She loved him. And she tried, she tried so hard to keep him. She took care of herself, she was good to his kids, she waited for him every night. What could be missing?

"Does she have anybody new in her life?" asked Joe.

"Nope. She's just got the kids. She's old, you know, like forty-five." Shawna wrinkled her nose.

"Well, there's your answer," said Joe confidently. "She's lonesome, so she might be trying to get him back, but you know she can't win. You already won, you're married to the guy."

"Yeah," Shawna said slowly. "But he has left his wife before."

And as Joe protested that the wife he left was the one she was worrying about, who was obviously therefore no threat, Shawna began to think. She had been so young when Alex began to flirt with her, to take her out, to sleep with her. Shawna knew that Alex was married, but he was so attractive, so into her, a doctor – and that just meant that they were supposed to be together. Shawna had seen lots of romantic comedies, and she knew for a fact that two people who desperately want to pull off each other's clothes should do whatever it takes to be together. That is the point of life, the happy ending. Sure, there might be some obstacles, a few people to step over or a few hilarious misadventures, but that was just part of the course of true love.

But wait, she thought slowly, maybe something was wrong with this picture. Maybe the romantic comedies hadn't considered all aspects of the situation. Now Shawna was the wife, and her life wasn't just happily ever after, fade to black. Just like Meredith's hadn't been. For a moment, Shawna saw that Meredith was a person, a woman who had been a wife, Alex's wife, and who had loved him and lost him, and who had cried and felt lonely. Meredith was a person, and Shawna had never considered her feelings for a single instant while she had slept with her husband and destroyed her marriage. But Shawna wasn't married to Meredith, she didn't owe her anything – did she?

Shawna shook herself and pushed back her glass. Well, maybe she should have considered Meredith's feelings a little before, but it was too late now. She certainly didn't owe Meredith her husband back. Maybe she had been young and blind and nudged Humpty Dumpty off the wall, but now he was broken, and no one could put him back together again. Things were different, Alex had married her, he loved her, and he was at the hospital, saving lives.

With a nod to Joe, Shawna grabbed her jacket and left the bar. She got into the BMW and drove as fast as she could to Evanston Hospital, where she zipped into a space reserved for emergency room patients, jumped out, and marched through the automatic double doors.

"I am Mrs. Alexander Bennett, and I want to see my husband, Dr. Alexander Bennett, right now," she announced to the young woman at the front desk.

"Oh, sure, Mrs. Bennett, come on in. We'll get him for you," the woman said.

The next set of double doors swooshed open, and Shawna stepped through into the Emergency Department, where she spotted Alex in his white coat, a stethoscope around his neck, hanging over a computer screen. The next thing she knew, she was hugging him. This was where she felt happy and safe, this was where she belonged. And Alex had been at work, of course he had. She had been crazy to imagine anything else.

"Why don't you come home, Alex, I miss you," she murmured. She spotted an unopened package of orange peanut butter crackers lying on the desk. "Poor guy, working so hard, never getting a decent meal. Come home with me." She ran her finger down his side. "I'll fix you something tasty."

"That's okay, don't worry, I ate with Meredith and the kids," he said distractedly. "You run along home, I'll be there in a bit."

Shawna turned and walked out the door. Of course she knew Alex had eaten with the kids in

Wilmette, he had told her his plans. But he hadn't said Meredith's name. And somehow, Shawna had convinced herself that Meredith might be somewhere else. Her heart ached painfully in her chest, and she stopped, resting her hand on the hospital's brick wall. What was she going to do about Meredith? Once, in a crazy scheme, Shawna had lied that she was pregnant, rubbing Meredith's face in her youth and fertility and sexual activity. But that hadn't worked. The lie had emerged, and its discovery had brought Alex and Meredith closer and isolated Shawna in her shame. Now she was desperate. She would have to try something else. This time, she might even have to try telling the truth.

Chapter Fourteen

It was 9:30 Monday morning, and Meredith needed to talk with Pamela Bigelow about the murder of her husband. After shepherding her children to their school buses, Meredith had leaped into the driver's seat of her Honda and headed toward Lake Shore Drive. Perched in the cup holder, her new cell phone stood ready to convey reports that Maggie had fled school despite last night's resolution, or that Lucy had vomited her Pop-Tart on the linoleum floor. This vigilance, as primal as breathing for most mothers, seemed absent from the interesting Pam. She had attempted the ultimate parental cop-out, in addition to possibly having killed her husband. Meredith parked, boarded the elevator in the Feinberg Pavilion of Northwestern Memorial Hospital, and then followed the signs down the hall to Room 1125. The heavy wooden door was ajar. Meredith knocked, eased it open, and walked in.

"Pamela Bigelow?" she asked.

"Yes?"

Pam pushed herself up to a taller sitting position with her right hand, her left hand limply dangling the taped needle of an IV line. Somehow she had scored a corner room – maybe to increase her will to live? Outside, the lake, gray-green and frisky, rushed playfully toward the feet of skyscrapers. Meredith glimpsed the marble face of the Ritz Hotel, which Pam had exited yesterday as the unconscious center of a flurry of activity. Although Northwestern Memorial tried to market itself as a Ritz of sorts, with its private rooms, upscale location, and chef-made meals, the catheters and unflattering sleepwear were tough obstacles to overcome. In addition, the word "memorial" in its name – why did hospitals do that? – constituted a subliminal reminder that these posh digs could be your last.

"Mrs. Bigelow, my name is Meredith Bennett. I'm an assistant state's attorney. I wanted to talk with you about – yesterday." Meredith studied Pam, collapsed in the rumpled bedding. Her face was pale, and stray strands of her streaked blonde hair splayed out on her pillow like a halo. Her plaid hospital gown hung askew from her thin frame to reveal a well-muscled arm. This woman did her exercises. Physically, she was stronger than she first appeared.

"Yes. I'm sorry. I hope I didn't cause too much trouble, but I know I did. I know I used up valuable resources, but I'll pay all my bills, the Ritz – please, I was just so upset. My husband …."

"What about your husband?"

"He left me, you see. For another woman. It's just so painful. I wasn't thinking straight." A tear slid down her cheek, and she clutched at the sheet with her IV'd hand. "But I won't do it again. I promise. If you could just give me another chance."

Meredith couldn't tell if Pam was confessing to Winston's murder, or if she had no idea that her husband was dead, and she thought she was about to be prosecuted for leaving the Ritz without properly checking out. Clearly, she thought that her husband was having an affair, a story that Meredith had not heard before, but which didn't surprise her much. It was possible that, considering her earlier unconsciousness and her precarious mental state, no one had told Pam that her husband was dead, and that she didn't know it -- unless, of course, she had killed him herself. She might have killed him – she was upset, she had fled the scene, she had tried to take her own life. Pam was a desperate woman who had been willing to leave her own child forever after impulsively exacting her revenge. Or, what if Pam deliberately had taken not quite enough medication, what if she had assumed that the maid would find her before she expired? She had, after all, chosen a hotel with twice-daily maid service. Maybe the suicide attempt was just a distraction, a play for sympathy by a manipulative, scorned woman. Meredith would have to find out.

"Mrs. Bigelow, I need to tell you something. It's about your husband. You are going to have to be strong. Can you do that? Do you want me to get a nurse?"

Pam's face melted into the pillow, and she cringed, like a dog waiting to be hit. "No, just tell me. How can things be any worse?"

"I'm sorry. Your husband is dead. He died early Sunday morning. He – was killed."

Pam gasped. Her left hand flew to her mouth and yanked the IV. She winced, and tears seeped from her eyes. "What happened?"

"He was sitting on a bench in Gillson Park. Someone came up behind him and strangled him with his scarf."

Pam started to choke, and her hands pushed on the middle of her chest. Meredith ran to the door and called for a nurse. "Come quickly. Mrs. Bigelow has had a shock."

And every indication was that she had indeed. Maybe she had killed Winston, but his death wasn't real to her until an outside source confirmed it. Or, could Pam have killed Winston and not known it? She might have pulled the scarf tight, tied it to the bench, and left while he was still struggling. Maybe it was a murder attempt, like her suicide attempt, not really meant to result in some Shakespearean family of corpses.

When Meredith re-entered the room, the nurse was smoothing Pam's hair into place. In an effort to regain her dignity, Pam scooted herself higher in the bent bed, but a pillow dislodged and fell over her right eye. The nurse gently leaned her forward, replaced the pillow, and stood straight. "Are you alright now?"

"Yes, thanks. You can go now. Thanks."

The nurse left, clogs clacking, and closed the door. "I'm sorry," said Meredith. "I know this is hard. I need to ask you a few questions." Pam nodded. "So, you didn't know about – Winston?"

"No. Look. Where is Ricky?"

So, now she was thinking about her son. It was Meredith's turn to blanch, since she did not, in fact, know where Ricky was. "Ricky is fine, we'll talk about him in a minute. What did you do on Saturday night?"

"Nothing – I mean, we had the parties at our house, the Turnabout parties, before and after the New Trier dance. Then, really late, Winston went for a walk. And then I – well, I stayed home for a while, and then I got in the car and drove around and ended up at the Ritz."

"You didn't follow Winston into the park?"

Pam flushed. "Of course not. It was freezing cold, and why would I want to follow him anyway?"

Why indeed, Meredith thought. "So, were all the kids gone when Winston left?"

"Yes – no – that is, there was a group of freshmen, friends of our son, and a group of seniors. The freshmen had left, but the seniors were still there. So I had to stay too."

"And where was Ricky?" Meredith asked. "Did he follow his father into the park?"

"Of course not!" Pam cried, looking genuinely alarmed. "He went to bed."

158

"Did you see him in bed?"

"Well, no, he's fourteen, I don't tuck him in. But I'm sure he went to bed."

"But there were a lot of comings and goings and there was a lot of noise and commotion."

Pam sat forward. "Are you seriously proposing that my young son killed his father? Are you kidding me?" she yelled.

Meredith decided to move on. "So you stayed home a while, and then you went for a drive. What time was that?"

"I don't really know. Maybe 4:00 a.m.? I was upset, I didn't check my watch."

"You were upset," said Meredith.

"Well, yes. You would have been too, if you had seen your husband with his girlfriend that night."

Meredith adjusted her glasses. "Yes, you said that he was leaving you for another woman. Was she at the party?" The Fishers had told her that Winston was leaving his law firm, but they hadn't said anything about his leaving his wife. Apparently this wasn't public knowledge.

"She certainly was, and it was very tacky. It was very hard to watch. She's one of his partners, and her daughters just happened to be at our party. Maybe that's why the seniors were there…." Puzzled, Pam shook her head. "All that so his – whatever -- could come over for a few minutes."

"One of his partners. What's her name?"

"Nicole Fisher. What a whore."

Yikes. Just when you thought you had moved to a nice neighborhood. Meredith pulled over a chair to buy time. "Nicole Fisher," Meredith said thoughtfully. "I believe I spoke with her in connection with this – situation. She didn't say anything about having an affair with your husband. How do you know that was going on? Did Winston tell you?"

"What do you think? They never do. Men are such assholes. Her husband told me. In Starbucks." Pam closed her eyes. Then she opened them. "Where's Ricky?"

Jeez Louise, the Fishers had lied to her, and she had no idea where Ricky was. Well, he must be at home or with friends. "When I saw Ricky, he was at home," Meredith said.

"Okay, then I need to get out of here and go to him. Wait, you saw him, does he know about his dad?"

"We didn't tell him, we thought you should do it. But that was yesterday. He may know by now."

"Oh my god, I have to get home, he must be so upset." Pam started to kick her feet out of the bed.

"Mrs. Bigelow, you need to talk with your doctor. Wait." Meredith put her hand on Pam's arm. Now Pam was acting like a mother. This was someone she recognized. "Let me get the nurse." She pushed the call button. "One more thing. Is there anyone you can think of who might have wanted to do this to Winston?"

160

Pam looked up. "Well, we were getting a lot of scary phone calls and threats. We were building a beach house, and the neighbors didn't like it."

"Enough to kill him?" Meredith asked.

"I don't know," said Pam. "I was scared. People are crazy. Nurse," she yelled into the air, "I want to go home now."

They certainly were. As the nurse came in, Meredith grabbed her coat and hurried out.

Angus barked excitedly as Ned pulled his leash off the hook in the front closet and attached it to his collar. Ned then put on his heavy coat, and the watchman's cap he wore to cover his ears in harsh winter weather. He wrapped the puckered scarf Eileen had knitted for him years ago, during her brief crafty phase, snuggly around his neck, and this time he tucked its fraying tails under his coat to prevent any misunderstandings with Angus. Ned had already tugged his boots over thick wool socks, and his gloves were in his coat pocket. Walking Angus was a fulltime job in February, but Ned was happy for the routine and the companionship after yesterday's shocking news.

Everyone on Michigan Avenue, and probably everyone in the village, knew that Winston Bigelow was dead. His name had been omitted from the newspaper story this morning, "pending notification of family

Ordinarily, Ned would have objected to this selfish attitude, but Ricky's awkward self-absorption touched him in some way. Ned remembered being a teenage boy, the discomfort of a body that kept extending and broadening when he most wanted to disappear. And Angus seemed to like him. The dog paced around the table, then paused while Ricky smiled to himself and scratched Angus's ears. Despite his ungainly size, Ricky was still a child. Ned took off his coat and tossed it onto the boy's lap. "Here, you look cold."

"Thanks," said Ricky, and to Ned's relief, he arranged the coat over his legs like a blanket.

"Where's your mom?" asked Ned. He would not mention Ricky's father, he was not going to deal with that.

"I don't know," Ricky said.

"Okay," said Ned. "It's lunchtime. Let's have some soup."

"Yeah," muttered Ricky, and he relaxed a little. "Can I use your bathroom?"

When Ricky came back, Ned poured hot tomato soup into two bowls. On second thought, he took a packet of saltines and splayed them in the middle of the table, and he set out a peanut butter jar with a knife stuck in it. They both sat down, and Ricky leaned forward eagerly, silently shoveling in spoonfuls of soup and stuffing in peanut butter crackers. Ricky was warming up, and he liked his lunch. Taking care of him wasn't that different from taking care of Angus. He just needed the basics right now. Ned felt competent, almost happy.

"So," he began, when Ricky leaned back. "What were you doing out there?"

"Sleeping," Ricky murmured. He met Ned's eyes and seemed to realize that he owed Ned something more. "I couldn't stay in the house. The phone was ringing all the time."

That made a sort of sense to Ned. He hated to answer the phone, who knew who was on the other end. Pests, that's all. "How long were you out there?"

"I don't know."

Ned wouldn't ask him about school or if he knew his father was dead. That wasn't his job. He would feed the boy and keep him safe. He would be a good neighbor, unlike whoever was calling, who would talk at him and slobber over him and boss him around.

"Do you want to watch TV?" Ned asked.

"Sure," said Ricky.

They put the dishes in the sink. Then they walked into the living room and sat down side by side, with Angus in the middle, staring at the screen.

Usually, by the time Maggie had waited through the line for her two tacos, side of corn, and fruit cup, the junior high cafeteria was teeming with noisy seventh graders shoveling in food and shouting to their friends.

Today, though, the room loomed in all its cavernous sterility, linoleum floors and concrete block walls and plastic tables in endless columns. Where was everybody? Maggie stood with her tray, frozen in indecision. The "cool" table to the right, where her former friend Stacy was now attempting to fit in, probably had some empty seats today. Stacy might not shoo her away if Maggie sat in her general vicinity. Ahead and to the left, she could see the peanut-free table, where Linda sat dissecting the tuna sandwich her mother had packed for her this morning. Maggie decided to stick to her plan. Averting her eyes from any possible glimpse of Stacy, Maggie marched herself to the empty space next to Linda and deposited her tray there.

"May I sit here?" Maggie asked, pulling out the chair.

Linda looked up, stunned. "Sure," she said. She pushed her glasses up on her nose. "I think you're in my science class."

"Yeah," said Maggie. "Hey, what did you think of Mrs. Taylor's dress today?"

"Yeah," said Linda. "How old is she, anyway? Like thirty-five?"

"Yeah," said Maggie. They both giggled. Maggie picked up a taco, and half the filling fell out of the back onto her blue tray. "Oops." They both laughed again.

A yellow tray appeared next to Maggie's. It contained an empty taco shell, an apple, and a cup of water. Stacy pulled out the chair and sat down. Linda suddenly became very absorbed in her carrot sticks.

"Seven B is on a field trip today. Most of my friends are in Seven B," Stacy explained, eyeing Maggie's chocolate milk. "You shouldn't drink that, it'll make you fat," she pronounced.

Maggie felt a prickle start in her chest and radiate down her arms. She wanted to slug Stacy, tip her off her chair, and stomp on her bony body. How dare she deposit herself here as if nothing had happened, after rejecting Maggie for weeks, because today she had no one better? How dare she offer her obnoxious, anorexic advice, as if they were still friends? The least Maggie should do is tell Stacy that her seat was taken, that all the seats were soon to be filled with extremely cool girls with a variety of life-threatening symbiotic food allergies. Do unto others as they do unto you, wasn't that it? Well, maybe not quite, but an eye for an eye, that sounded like the rule of some mean king somewhere in world history. But that was fair, and Stacy should learn her lesson.

Next to her, Maggie could see Stacy's thin, white hands methodically breaking off pieces of taco shell and crumbling them onto her tray. Her apple, on its side, looked bruised and unwell. "You know, I took this yogurt, but I don't think I can eat it. Would either of you like it?" she asked casually. "It's low fat."

"I'm good," said Linda, "I've got one already."

"Well – if you're just going to waste it…" said Stacy.

"I totally am," said Maggie. She placed the yogurt on Stacy's tray.

They heard a big ruckus of stomping feet and surging voices as Team Seven B flooded into the cafeteria and emptied their bag lunches onto the table tops. Stacy immediately stood, grabbed her tray, and rushed to the cool table. Smiling ingratiatingly, she elbowed her way to a seat beside Emma Reardon, who turned her sleek, well-tended twelve-year-old self slightly away.

"You want a cookie?" asked Linda. "They're chocolate chip."

"Thanks," said Maggie, settling back in her seat and resuming her lunch. "Did your mom make them? They look really good."

"Stacy is an idiot," murmured Linda.

"Yeah," said Maggie. They both giggled.

Chapter Fifteen

Once the nurse took out her IV, Pam was out of there. Oh, certainly, she knew she needed to be evaluated by psychiatric services. Of course her doctor needed to discharge her. Bloody hell. Pam was not waiting around for that red tape. She was fine, maybe a little woozy and nauseous, but anyone would be after what she'd been through in the last 36 hours. Bottom line, Ricky needed her. She was going home to her family. She was going to take care of her son.

Thank goodness she had attempted suicide at the Ritz. The concierge had sent her coat and purse to her hospital room. They had even shined her boots. Breezing past hospital security was so much easier in her cashmere winter gear than in bare feet and a tartan hospital gown, with her rear end popping out the back. The Ritz valet didn't say anything about her bill when she retrieved the Mercedes. Maybe they comped suicidal guests as an added service, though she doubted it. They had probably charged her credit card yesterday, just in case she died.

Pam rolled down the car's front windows. The February wind would clear her head. As she sped north, the lake seethed beside her, a churning presence. She could have rowed a boat home, she had never thought of that. But the traffic was moving well, it was early Monday afternoon. Obeying the green arrow, she turned onto Sheridan Road.

So, her husband was dead, murdered in the park. She had to make funeral arrangements. Or maybe she didn't, maybe the police wouldn't release his body for a while. Did she need to put an obituary in the paper, something about what a great husband and father he was? But that's not how it worked. Winston didn't belong to her and Ricky in life or in death. He was a major partner at the great Winters & Early. The law firm would handle his obituary, mention his clients, Bank of Whoever and Somebody's Capital Investments, maybe throw in a few war stories about a closing argument he had made or some time he hadn't changed his clothes for three days. She and Ricky would be lucky to score the last line. The firm's event planner might put together a memorial service for Winston – something tasteful, with a power point presentation and some light hors d'oeuvres. The speaker might mention that Winston was leaving the firm to pursue philosophy – oh, wasn't that just like him, such a deep man, a few warm chuckles, a few discreet tears. But he wouldn't mention that Winston was going to leave his family. He wouldn't say it, because he wouldn't know it, Winston didn't announce that. Oh god, who was she kidding? Winston was having an affair with a woman at work. Everyone there probably knew it. They would all be laughing at her, or pitying her. Or thinking that she had killed him.

Well, she wasn't going to worry about that now. She needed to take care of her son, to tell him that she was here now, someone he could depend on. In a way, it was easier that Winston was dead. Ricky might not see it that way at first, but ex-husband Winston would have been a problem. Either he would have wanted to see Ricky, and she would have had to deal with him, a constant reminder of his unfaithfulness – or he would have ignored Ricky, which was worse. This was clean. Winston was gone, and they had to move on. They could do what they liked with the villa. They could tear down the beach house and have friends again. She would inherit a lot of money too. Maybe they would move away from the lake and back to a real neighborhood, and she could use the money to set up her own yoga studio.

Pam turned onto Michigan and then, bouncing from the brick street to the cobblestone pavers, into her own driveway. The house looked the same, no signs of activity, no yellow police tape. She opened the front door. Everything was quiet. She listened for the sound of the TV, or of Ricky narrating some play-by-play to a video game or during one of his interminable showers. Nothing – just an eerie silence. She walked through the living room into the kitchen. Party refuse was around, some empty bottles and used glasses, though members," but some kids who knew him had found his body in the park on Sunday, and of course they couldn't keep their little traps shut. So buzz buzz buzz, all the phone lines in Wilmette flashed red, and before you could say, "none of your damned business," Mrs. Goldblatt had stopped him in front of her house and told him the news, as if he didn't know already. Of course the neighbors had seen the police going over the house and the yard, and they had been questioned, and everyone hated Winston, so it all added up.

Ned shut the front door after Angus and picked his way down the icy front steps to the driveway. Yes, everyone hated Winston for building that stupid beach house. But were they happy he was dead? Now his squeamish little wife would probably drop the whole thing, level what had been built and return the yard to nature – according to Mrs. Blah Blah Goldblatt, that's what everyone was saying, and they were happy about that – but no one would admit to being happy that Winston was dead. That would be crass and unfeeling. But what was the difference really? No one had liked him, and their lives would be better without him. Whoever had killed Winston had done a public service. Just no one had the guts to say so.

Ned walked around his house to the back. He saw the lake every day, and every day it amazed him. In the summer it could be cool and glassy, summoning him with a wet finger to wade in and feel the its chill. When he took off his shoes and paddled along the shore, he felt like a boy again. But looking out over its vastness all the way to the curved horizon, he felt his mortality, his insignificance. On this winter's day, the water roiled powerfully, awesome and spectacular. Ned stooped and let Angus off the leash. The dog wouldn't leap into the water today, it was freezing, but he liked to run on the damp sand and snoop in the dune grasses.

Ned tried to avert his eyes from the half-constructed beach house lurking on the periphery of his vision, but it was no use, it was like a car wreck, or a sore you had to pick at. As he nosed persistently along the beach, Angus felt the same attraction, for before long he was sniffing its stone bottom and circling its base. And then he disappeared.

"Angus, come back," Ned called. He did not want to step into the Bigelow yard. The police might come and see his footprints, or maybe he would shed a few hairs or threads there, and the next thing would be him in jail making one phone call to – who would even bail him out? Guilty conscience, his mother would have said, what do you have to hide? Just like his lie about Neighborhood Watch. Of course he had been out Saturday night, he was on the schedule, it was his duty – but he didn't need to give the police any extra ammunition. Everyone knew he had a feud with Winston. He wasn't going to add opportunity to motive.

But Angus didn't come back, and Ned had to go after him. From the doorway, he could hear the dog scuffing around and making little yips. The lake was behind him, and suddenly, a frozen breeze slapped his back and shoved him inside. Angus trotted up to Ned, and what he saw made his chest twist.

In the corner, away from the doorway, slumped a teenage boy. He was wearing a sweatshirt with the hood pulled up, shadowing his face. His bare legs curled into the sand, his big man's sneakers emerging puppyish from beneath him. Ned looked for a scarf around his neck, but there was no scarf. Angus ran back to the boy and licked his knee. The boy twitched, shivered, and sat up straight.

It was the Bigelow boy, and he was alive. With embarrassment, Ned realized that he didn't know his name. "Son, get up, are you all right?" he barked, trembling with the shock of thinking for a moment that the boy was dead. The boy just sat there. "Come on, stand up, we've got to get you inside. How long have you been out here, you must be freezing." Ned put his hand on the boy's shoulder, and he used the half-built wall to help him up. The boy was fully dressed, but for a mild April day, in shorts and a University of Illinois sweatshirt. That was where Ned had gone to college, where he had met Eileen. "What's your name, Son?" he asked gruffly.

"Ricky," the boy said, and they helped each other into the back door of Ned's house, with Angus leading the way.

In the kitchen, Ricky immediately dropped onto one of the dinette chairs at the kitchen table. He slouched, his head back, his legs sticking out in front.

mysteriously less than before -- but no evidence of Ricky – no dirty lunch plates, no frozen pizza boxes thrown in the sink. Outside, through the French doors, the lake lapped closer as the waves foamed and collapsed.

"Ricky, I'm home," she called.

No one answered, but he wouldn't. Pam glanced down at the blinking answering machine on the counter. Twenty-six messages. The doorbell rang. Throwing off her coat, she ran to answer it.

"Ah, Pam, you're back. I wanted to say how sorry I am. This is for you."

Looming in the doorway, Michael Fisher, dressed dashingly in a black turtle neck sweater and a blue blazer, thrust a foil casserole dish toward Pam's chest. Startled, she took a step back, permitting him to enter the house and kick the door closed. "It's lasagna. Don't worry, I didn't make it. Heating instructions are on the bottom, I'm told. Though maybe you don't eat pasta?" He looked concerned.

"Where did you come from – have you been watching me?" Pam asked.

"Don't be ridiculous. We saw, um, what's-her-name, the prosecutor, yesterday, and she said you were missing. I just dropped by a few times on my way back from Starbucks. The lasagna's been in the trunk of my car since yesterday. Nice thing about February – automatic ice box. Auto-matic – get it?" Michael grinned.

"Look, thanks for thinking of me, but I'm busy right now." She looked nervously toward the stairs. If Ricky were up there, she wasn't sure if she wanted him to come down or hide.

"Nonsense," Michael intoned expansively. "Here, let me put this in the fridge for you." He swept back into the kitchen, where he deposited the container on the island and tossed his jacket onto a stool. "This is a beautiful place. You should have seen the dump that was here before. We didn't even have a granite island in the kitchen. It was very hard to function," he murmured confidentially. "And I'm sure you find the warming drawer and the pasta arm absolutely vital, with all the large meals you whip up. What do you have – one child? But you must entertain a lot, your husband is such an important man. Oops, sorry, I forgot, he's dead. Hope I didn't hit a nerve."

"Michael," said Pam, keeping the island between them, "I don't know why you're angry at me. I'm a victim, just like you. My husband cheated on me, and now he's dead. Nothing is my fault."

Michael stopped to think. For a moment he looked genuinely puzzled, as if hostility had just become a habit, and he had forgotten that, while some people might have earned it, others might deserve his empathy. Then he shook his head, as if banishing a fog. "No, you're wrong. It takes two people to make a bad marriage – I read that in 'Dear Abby.' And one of them wasn't me. So it must be you. You weren't a very good wife, were you?"

Pam looked hard at Michael. "I don't know. I tried. Winston was gone a lot. Maybe he was bored with me, or maybe he just thought he was too important for me. But what he did was wrong. He hurt me. He should have been faithful, and he should have been honest. You know what I mean."

Michael met her eyes. "You're right. I do know." He walked around the island and put his hand on her shoulder. "We have a lot in common. Maybe you and I should be together."

"That's very nice," said Pam steadily, "but Winston just died. He was my husband, even if he was – flawed."

"And dumping you," added Michael.

"Yes," said Pam. "You knew he was having an affair, but how did you know he was leaving me?"

"Lucky guess," said Michael. "He was?"

"Yeah, to shack up with your wife. That philosopher stuff was bullshit, and your wife is a slut."

Maybe Pam shouldn't have said that. Michael grabbed both her arms and started to shake her. "This is all your fault. We were fine. We were managing. It was once with a stranger, that's all it was, and she would do anything to make it up to me. She quit her job, she stayed home with the girls, she made my dinner. But it wasn't a stranger, it was your husband. It's all his fault, it's all your fault."

Pam thought of Ricky, and she thought of yoga. She composed and centered herself spiritually, she felt the strength in her mind, in her core, and in her limbs. She summoned the power of eastern and western gods, of nature, and of her own soul. She anchored her left leg, flexed her right leg, and thrust her knee directly into Michael's groin. Immediately, he dropped her and fell to the floor in a fetal position. Pam grabbed the phone.

"I have an intruder at 1238 Michigan Avenue. It's the Bigelow residence. Please come quickly."

Leaving Michael on the kitchen floor, Pam hurried to the front door and stepped outside. All this commotion had certainly been enough to rouse anyone anywhere in the house, even a fourteen-year-old boy overdosing on Mario. What was she thinking, she had lost track of time, it was the middle of Monday afternoon. Ricky must be at school. Thank goodness, Ricky was safe at school.

"Okay if I take Angus out back?" Ricky asked. He was tired of TV. Incredibly, Ned did not have cable, he had like, five channels, and they were all showing soap operas or really lame talk shows. One of the hosts was kind of good looking, and Ricky had watched her for a while, but pretty soon he was just petting Angus and staring out the window. And once that happened, he started worrying again.

Ricky hadn't seen his parents since Saturday night, and now it was Monday afternoon. The police had come on Sunday, at least he thought they had, he had been awfully tired and maybe a little hung over after trying not to look like a total dork when the seniors showed up with all that beer. He had hated that party, he had hated everything about it, and he barely knew his date. Why did she even ask him to that dumb dance, maybe she had run out of boys or somebody had dared her. All he wanted the whole night was to go to his room and play video games. At least the freshmen finally left, and he could go upstairs. And he shouldn't complain. At least he had parents then.

"Sure, thanks." Ned looked up from the TV. "But it's cold out there. Go home and get a coat for yourself. You can take Angus with you."

What the heck had happened to his mother? Ricky walked out Ned's back door and into the yard, with Angus trotting behind, and then ahead. He went to bed on Saturday night, and on Sunday he woke up an orphan. Well, maybe his life wouldn't be so different. His father had always worked nonstop, and his mother had her own junk to do, whatever that was. Buy groceries and stuff. They didn't play with him, and anyway, he was too old now, though at one time he would have liked it. And all they said to him was blah blah math test, blah blah your grades – they didn't care about him at all, he was just supposed to do tricks for them, like some trained dog.

Ricky followed Angus close to the water. It was damn freezing out here, Ned was right, but he didn't feel like going home for a coat, or anything else. Why did they have to move to this awful house, they were fine before. His father liked living in the fanciest neighborhood, but there were no kids here, just a bunch of old people. And the house was a tomb. Ricky missed his old street, where at least somebody might be outside throwing a ball, and the lady next door had a couple cats that would show up on their porch, and he would feed them turkey slices from a plastic tub. Ricky threw a stick to Angus, who fetched it back to Ricky and sniffed his leg. He was so tired of being alone. Most kids had a brother or a sister – even if they were annoying, it was somebody – and most kids had a dog, or at least a cat or a lizard. Ricky had nothing. Dogs were too much work, and Ricky's mother didn't want to deal with it, like she had anything else to do. His parents were selfish, old and selfish, that's all.

But now they were gone. How could they just disappear, without saying anything? Maybe they were in a car accident, and they were dead, and no one was telling him. That's probably why the police came, and why Ned was being nice to him now. Ricky didn't think his life could get any sadder, that he could feel any more alone, but dead parents were the worst. His grandmother lived in Indiana, maybe he would get sent to her. But who would even send him? And he didn't want to go, her house smelled like cough syrup. He could live with his friends, if he had any. He palled around with a couple guys at school, of course he did, he wasn't a loser, but he didn't know anyone well enough to move in.

Ricky threw the stick back to Angus, but this time it landed in the lake. The stick bobbed on the edge, and then the waves picked it up, flipped it around, and set it back on the sand. Angus ran up to grab it, but he didn't like stepping into the cold water. They stood together, watching the stick wash back into the waves, dancing it farther and farther out. Angus looked up at Ricky. His eyes were warm and brown and trusting. The dog was the closest thing Ricky had to a family right now, and that was pathetically, pitifully sad.

For some reason he took off his shoes. It was just a habit, it just seemed right, to take off your shoes before going into the water. He took a step in. Damn, it was cold, and in a moment it wasn't only cold, it was pure pain. The waves surged up, and he ran into them, absurdly trying to keep warm. The stick had been just out of reach when he entered, but it kept sliding back, up and down the waves, but always near the surface, like it was skiing. Ricky had never gone skiing, his parents weren't interested in taking him, and now he would never go, he thought, but that was okay. The pain was terrible, but he had no choice but to go on. Maybe if he dove in, he would get used to it, and the pain would stop. And he wouldn't have to know that his parents had left him alone. Now they would know what it felt like to be left alone for good. The last thing Ricky heard before he went under was Angus, barking on the shore.

As he rinsed out the soup bowls from lunch and stacked them in the dishwasher, Ned caught himself humming. He knew it was wrong, with Winston Bigelow dead and Ricky's life in shambles, but he was enjoying his afternoon. Now that Winston was dead, the beach house construction would be, at the very least, delayed. Ned hadn't realized how heavily the constant concern and the responsibility to harass had weighed on him, and now that it was gone, he felt his mood lighten. And spending some time with Ricky, warming him up and feeding him, well, that had helped them both. Ned remembered his own son Bill at that age, so awkward and sullen. Heck, he had been that way himself a million years ago, and he knew just to let it ride, to be a solid, uncritical presence. Maybe after Ricky's mother came back, he would still come by sometimes, just to watch TV or play with Angus. Where was that woman? She must be out of her tree, abandoning her son like that.

Ned looked up, toward the kitchen window. Outside, Angus was barking furiously and dashing up and down the dunes between the house and the lake. Ned peered past the sand, and in the water, bouncing in the frigid waves, he thought he saw a brown head surfacing and submerging. Oh my god. He grabbed the

180

phone and punched in 911. Immediately, he heard sirens, as a police car, a fire truck, and an ambulance arrived next door, at the Bigelow house. Ned ran outside, screaming for help.

Chapter Sixteen

Earning two minutes on the local news for heroism and a special commendation from the Village, two fire fighters dove into the icy water of Lake Michigan and pulled Ricky Bigelow to shore. The paramedics revived him, loaded him into one of the two ambulances now parked on the block, and raced to Evanston Hospital. When Meredith arrived at the Bigelow residence, an anxious Pam was pacing the kitchen, while police officers Brad Wood and Dan O'Brien questioned a subdued Michael Fisher.

"Thanks," Meredith said, nodding to the policemen. "Mrs. Bigelow, please sit down."

Pam and Meredith pulled out kitchen chairs for themselves at the table where Michael slouched, his legs splayed straight in front of him. He had mounted an ice pack on top of his groin with belligerent indiscretion. Despite his challenging stare, he looked pale and slightly queasy.

"So, Mr. Fisher," Meredith began, pulling a pen and a notebook from her briefcase, "what are you doing here?"

"Just bringing a casserole to the grieving widow. Is that illegal?"

"Only if, in the process, you assault her. And why would you make a condolence call on Mrs. Bigelow?"

"Let's just say that we have a lot in common. Let's see – I've slept with my wife Nicole, and Pam has slept with her husband Winston, and Nicole and Winston have slept together. I think that makes Pam and me – cousins? Spouses once removed?" Michael looked up at Pam and then shifted his ice pack.

"I just want to get to the hospital to see Ricky," Pam blurted. "Can you please ask me what you need so I can get out of here?"

Meredith turned to Pam, who looked coiled tight and ready to spring. "Of course. Let's go into the living room."

Pam was a suspect in her husband's murder. She had the motive and the opportunity to kill him, and she had behaved erratically since his death. But she loved her son. Would she really have left him alone for two days – and possibly forever, if her suicide attempt had succeeded -- knowing that his father was dead? Meredith didn't think so, but she couldn't be sure. And the tied scarf, creating uncertainty about whether the killer knew that Winston was dead when he or she left, was an additional complication.

"I'm glad to see you're feeling better," Meredith began. "We need to discuss Saturday night again. Did you take a walk in the park after Winston left the house?"

The doorbell rang, an unnerving clang echoing off the marble floors. Pam paused, while Officer Wood left to answer it. In a moment he returned with Ned Haskell from next door. Pam jumped up from the couch and ran to him.

"Thank you, thank you." She reached out and grabbed his arms and started to weep. "You saved my son. Thank god for you, I'll never be able to repay you. That beach house – it's gone, I promise you. Anything – I can't thank you enough for saving my child."

"It's fine, really. I'm glad I could help." Ned looked at Pam, and his brow furrowed. "He's a nice young man."

"Thank you for saying so," Pam sobbed. "I worry about him. He doesn't talk to me much. And now, his father is gone – a boy needs a father, even a lousy one like Winston."

"Mrs. Bigelow, please sit down," Meredith said, trying to keep some control over the situation. "Mr. Haskell, why don't you sit too, for a minute." She pointed to a chair, which he took. "What brings you here?"

"Well, when I came out front to get help, I saw your car." He nodded to Pam. "I spent some time with Ricky today. He's a nice boy, maybe a little mixed up now. I wanted to see you for myself. That boy – do you know I found him outside this morning, half frozen?" Pam hung her head and began to cry again. "But now I see you – I think you love your son. He needs you. You can't just leave, that boy needs you."

Pam looked up at Ned. "I know. I was half crazy. I see that now."

"And I need to tell you something," Ned said, turning to Meredith. "I'm afraid that I wasn't completely – candid – about Saturday night."

"Go on," said Meredith.

"Well, if I change my story – that wasn't perjury, was it, do I need immunity? I can't go to jail, I have a dog."

"Don't worry. Just tell me what happened."

"Okay. I was on Neighborhood Watch that night," said Ned. "Normally I wouldn't be out at three or four in the morning, but there was a lot of racket from the party next door, loud music, cars coming and going, and I was worried that a gang of drunken teenagers might – I don't know, break windows, drive up on someone's lawn, who knows, but I couldn't sleep, that's the point. So I went outside to patrol the area, and who should I see walking down the block, but Pam, here."

"Ned, you told us before that you didn't leave the house."

"I know, that's what I'm telling you. I know it was wrong, I just didn't want to stir up any trouble. I figured you'd know I had a problem with Winston and the beach house, and I didn't want you to think I'd gone outside and killed him." He laughed nervously. "So if I just said I had stayed in, you'd know for sure that I didn't kill him – which is the truth, I swear, the last part, I mean."

"All right, so you say you saw Mrs. Bigelow walking down the block. Was she heading toward the park?" Meredith asked.

"Yes, she was."

"And how did you know it was Mrs. Bigelow?"

Michael strode into the living room and plopped his ice pack on the coffee table. "This has been quite a treat, but can I go?"

"Well, that depends," said Meredith. "Mrs. Bigelow, do you want to press charges against Mr. Fisher?"

Pam glared at Michael. "I've got enough problems," she said, "as long as he'll agree to stay away from me." She stood and faced him. "I haven't done anything to you, do you get that?" she yelled.

"I do, I get it. Sorry," he said. "Can I go?"

"Yes," said Meredith, "if the officers are done with you." She could deal with him later, things were already complicated enough here. Michael picked up his jacket and sauntered out the front door, and then slammed it with a thud. "Okay, Mr. Haskell. How did you recognize Mrs. Bigelow walking toward the park in the middle of the night? You've said you don't know her very well."

"I was already outside, and I saw her walk down her driveway. I was right across the street. It was Pam, I'm sure of it." Ned nodded vigorously.

Meredith turned to Pam. "You told me that you stayed home and then went for a drive Saturday night. Is there anything you would like to add?"

"Not yet," said Pam, coloring slightly.

"I also knew it was Pam because I followed her, and at the end, she went back into her house," said Ned.

Meredith sat forward. "You followed her. Why did you do that?"

"Well, I thought it was terrible, irresponsible, you know, that she was taking a stroll in the middle of the night while she had a house full of out-of-control teenagers. And it was cold outside, it didn't make sense. I wanted to see what she was up to. She went into the park and walked down the sidewalk along the lakefront."

"Did you see Winston Bigelow?" Meredith asked excitedly. If Ned were telling the truth, this could be it.

"I think so. I saw the back of a man sitting on a park bench. Mrs. Bigelow here saw him too. She stopped a few feet behind him and stared, anyway. And then she left. She didn't talk to him, she didn't do anything, she just turned around and walked back the way she came. I followed her out of the park and saw her return to her house. Then I went home. It had gotten a lot quieter – lord knows what the teenagers were doing at that point, I don't even want to think about it, alone in that house with no supervision. And I was exhausted. I went to bed and fell asleep." Maybe the kids had already left for the park, Meredith thought. If they had walked along the sand instead of the sidewalk, Ned and Pam would not have seen them.

"Mr. Haskell, was the man you saw on the bench alive when you and Mrs. Bigelow left him?" asked Meredith.

"He was," said Ned firmly. "He was sitting pretty still, and the light was dim, but when Pam walked away, he turned his head a little. He didn't turn around, then he would have seen her." Ned paused. "If he'd seen her, maybe none of this would have happened. But he reacted to the sound, I'm almost sure of it."

"Did you notice if his scarf was knotted around the back of the bench?"

"No, I don't think it was. That would be odd, and I don't remember anything strange like that," said Ned. "Though I will admit that the light wasn't good. But I am completely certain that Pam here did not kill her husband, not on my watch. And I didn't either," he added.

Meredith turned to Pam. "Your neighbor here seems to have given you an alibi, if you were in fact in the park that night. Were you?"

"I'm sorry," Pam said. "I just didn't see what good could come of my telling you. I knew it would look bad, and I didn't kill Winston. I just wanted to see what he was doing, whether he was meeting – someone. But he wasn't. He was just thinking, I guess. He was just sitting there, alone in the dark, and thinking." She paused. "You know, Winston never told me that he slept with someone else. Michael told me. Maybe he wasn't leaving me for Nicole Fisher, maybe he told me the truth, he just needed to be alone, to think about life." Pam turned to Meredith. "But he was still leaving me and Ricky. Does that noble-sounding reason make him any less of a jerk? And can I go now?"

Meredith smiled slightly. "Just one more minute, please. What happened when you saw Winston sitting there, on the bench?"

Pam thought for a moment. "I was embarrassed that I had followed him to the park, and I was so angry at him. But I didn't talk to him. I guess I was waiting for him to notice me, to say something. When he didn't, I just left. I do think he was alive then. I would never have left Ricky alone if I had known his father was dead, you've got to know that."

Meredith did not respond. Leaving a bunch of teenagers unattended and then attempting suicide was hardly exemplary maternal behavior, whether she thought her son's father was alive or not. "When you returned to the house, what time was it?"

"I'm not sure, maybe four?"

"And was the party still going on?"

"No," said Pam. "The kids had left. It was quiet, so I checked the basement. Can I go now?"

"Yes," said Meredith. "I hope Ricky is doing well."

"I can't believe he walked into that frigid water," Pam said. "What on earth was he thinking?"

Seems like a chip off the old block, thought Meredith, but she didn't say it. Pam was suffering enough. But if she and Ned were telling the truth at last, Meredith would have to look elsewhere for Winston's murderer.

Chapter Seventeen

"Girls, I thought I'd just order some pizza for dinner. Is that okay with you?" Nicole pushed open her daughters' bedroom door and stepped inside.

"Sure, Mom, whatever," Abby said, looking up from some equations scrawled in a spiral notebook. On the neighboring bed, Kelsey, who was painting her toenails green while bouncing to her Discman, appeared neither to have heard nor seen her mother. "I'm sure Kelsey agrees," said Abby, returning to her calculus homework.

Silently surveying the twins' bedroom, Nicole tried to relax and appreciate the pleasure of having them home doing their after-school teenage things. In a few months, this would be over. The girls would pack their favorite pillows and stuffed bears and maybe even the matching pink floral comforters that they had snuggled under since junior high into brown cardboard boxes, and off they would go to University of Whatever, presumably two different colleges, considering their different proclivities. When they came home for Christmas, they would be guests in their own home, catered to and endured in hopes that they would want to return for future visits. Eighteen years had passed, first glacially slowly, and then, once they had started school, with alarming speed, time ticked off in semesters and school breaks and summer vacations, until now, it was almost gone. Soon they would be walking in their white graduation dresses to the drone of "Pomp and Circumstance," one hand clutching the arm of a white tuxedoed male senior, the other holding a single red rose. And although Nicole joked that New Trier seemed to be summoning five hundred virgins to the rim of a volcano, this did feel a little like a death to her.

"Mom, anything else?" Abby asked. "You're starting to freak me out."

"Where's Dad?" Kelsey pulled her headphones down to rest on her neck. She was wearing plaid pajama bottoms and a sleeveless white tee shirt of a type more commonly seen on plumbers immersed in toilets. Nicole prayed that Kelsey had not worn this outfit to school today.

"He's at work," Nicole said. For this morning, after a weekend of lunatic behavior, Michael had showered and combed his hair and pulled on some khaki slacks and a blue blazer. Granted, he had left the house a little late – actually, it was after lunch – but he had dressed appropriately and, after consuming a routine bowl of Cheerios, exited in a businesslike manner. Nicole was determined to see this as a return to normality. At work, the demands of Michael's law practice would distract him and begin the process of washing his brain of the horrors of the weekend. Perhaps not today, but sometime in the next few weeks, he would sit down with her, take her hand, and announce that he had processed the situation, and he was hoping that Nicole would join him on the train to Winters & Early. He would say that he understood, that he forgave her, and that he loved her more than anything. He just needed a little more time.

"Mom." Abby looked at her pointedly.

"Sorry. I'm gone," Nicole said, walking out of the bedroom and leaving the door ajar.

In the kitchen, Nicole phoned Giordano's for delivery of a large stuffed spinach pizza. Glancing out the window as she ordered, she noticed a few snowflakes starting to fall. Usually Nicole had a handle on the weather, or at least the weather report, but, with all the upheaval of the last 48 hours, she realized that she had no idea whether these pretty white wisps were a momentary distraction or the beginnings of a blizzard. After years in Chicago, she was well beyond experiencing any delight in watching white puffs floating in the air or lining tree branches. They only made her think of impassable streets, the chore of shoveling, and slipping on the ice and breaking her wrist. She felt a little guilty ordering the pizza delivery guy to drive out in bad weather, but that was why she paid him the big bucks, she thought, removing seven dollars from her wallet and slipping the money into her pants pocket.

The least she could do as a decent mom was make a salad. Nicole opened the refrigerator door, and as she rifled through plastic packages of browning prewashed lettuce, she felt a gentle hand on her behind. "What's for dinner?" Michael asked, in an eerily tender voice.

Nicole stood, a bag of limp romaine in one hand, a cucumber in the other, and shut the refrigerator door. "Michael. I didn't hear you come in. We're having pizza. I'm tired today," she said, turning to examine her husband's face and demeanor. His jacket collar flapped up messily, and his chin was stubbly where he had missed a spot this morning. She felt something vaguely predatory emanating from him, a tension and heat. She took a step back.

"No home-cooked meal for the breadwinner today?" he asked.

"How was work?" she countered. "You couldn't have been there long."

He paused, considering. "I'm not going to lie to you, Nicole. I'm not a liar – like some people. I decided not to go to work today. I went to see Pam Bigelow. I brought her a lasagna," he said, smiling slightly to himself.

"That was – nice," said Nicole, though she doubted it. "So. Why did you do that?"

"Nicole, I'm surprised at you -- grieving widow and all that, we're practically neighbors, they live in our old – space – and we were all partners, with Winston I

194

mean. That is a sacred trust, partnership, it comes with its ethical responsibilities and a certain – friendship -- almost like a marriage."

"Michael, I'm sick of this crap. I know you're mad at me, I get that, and I'm sorry. I'm really sorry, you know that. And it was Winston, but it could have been a man from Mars. I was drunk and did the stupidest thing of my life. But you've got to man up and get over it. I'm sorry, and Winston is dead." She took another step back. For the first time since they had moved to this house, she wished she had an island in the kitchen, so she could put it between them.

"That is a neat and tidy package, isn't it? But for some reason, I just couldn't put it behind me right away, even after Winston's death. I felt like there was some dangling participle – you know, the gnawing feeling of something left undone, something unnamed, that you just can't put your finger on. Well, it's not a good feeling, it eats at you, you'll do just about anything to resolve the situation, to make yourself whole." He shook his head. "For some reason, I thought Pam was the missing link. Then she disappeared, and I couldn't see her. It was very unsettling. But she came back today, and I was there, right behind her." Michael pursed his lips prissily. He looked pleased with himself.

"So – what happened?" Nicole was almost afraid to ask, but he had brought lasagna – how bad could it be?

"Well, we had a bit of a skirmish, but it was good, it was very illuminating. You see, I realized that I was blaming the wrong person."

"What do you mean?"

Michael took a step toward Nicole. "Well, as I said, even after Winston's death, I still didn't feel – satisfied. I know, I should have taken hold of myself, I should have said, 'Michael, the man who screwed your wife, who destroyed your home, who degraded and patronized you, and who has stolen your life – he is dead. Revenge can't get much better than that – no matter how he died. But I just couldn't shake the feeling that something remained undone. And I thought, Pam, she's the key – really, this is her fault. I know it sounds crazy, she wasn't even at the Polynesian Resort – but she was married to Winston, they must have been some kind of corrupt couple, like Mr. and Mrs. Macbeth."

"But she's a housewife – she's nothing," said Nicole.

"Exactly," said Michael. "You've always been so good at cutting to the heart of the matter, with no niceties or complexities to clutter up the picture. I think that is why you are such a good litigator, so much better than I could ever be. She was just a dumb cluck little housewife – how could all of the high level machinations at the Polynesian Resort have anything to do with the likes of her?"

Nicole thought she heard the front door close, and she glanced toward the stairs. Michael was getting loud, and his arms were tense, poised. "Calm down, Honey. We can talk about this," she murmured, as she brushed by him to walk into the living room. Michael grabbed her arm.

"It's you, you are the problem," he yelled. "You are the person I can't get out of my mind! Everywhere I go, it's you – you in the bar, flirting and flipping your skirt around, you in the elevator hugging and laughing, you in the bedroom, with your dress, without your dress, I can't even say it. In vino veritas, the drinks were just an excuse, you wanted to have sex with Winston, someone powerful and rich and – someone who wasn't me!"

Michael gripped Nicole tightly and jerked her toward him, as she tried to pull away. He clenched both her arms, and his eyes burned. "I loved you! Winston was a shit, but Winston owed me nothing. I loved you, we had a family together, we built a life together, and you treated me like garbage!"

"I'm sorry," said Nicole, starting to cry. "I wasn't thinking about you, it didn't have anything to do with you."

"How can you say that? We are married, you promised me – how could I not be in your head when you were having sex with someone else?"

Michael started to shake her violently. Nicole didn't care anymore what the girls heard, she had to protect herself, it was instinctive, she started to scream. Michael moved one hand over her mouth and held her tightly against himself with the other, his hand behind her neck, his arm pushing against her back. "I thought maybe I could have sex with Pam," he seethed, "and then you would see what it feels like. But that didn't happen, I didn't even want to, and I'm so angry at you, you're torturing me, and I don't know what to do --."

The front door opened, and Meredith rushed in, followed by Abby and Kelsey. They had snowflakes in their hair. In the distance, Nicole could hear a siren, coming closer.

"Michael, let go of her," Meredith said firmly. Nicole could feel him clutching her closer. She could barely breathe. "The police will be here in a moment. Don't make things worse."

"Dad, please," Abby pleaded, and then she and Kelsey did something amazing. They stepped behind their father, and they put their arms around him. Michael let go of Nicole. He put his face in his hands and started to cry. Both girls remained where they were, hugging their father.

"I'm sorry," he said. "I didn't mean to do it. I was so upset. I was walking in the park, trying to clear my head. I thought I might see my girls, after their dance, I just wanted to see you, I knew you were coming to the park. But instead, I saw him, sitting on the bench. He looked so peaceful, it wasn't fair. I walked up behind him, he didn't seem to hear me. He could have escaped. All he had to do was turn around and look at me. All he had to do was see me. But he didn't do it. I touched his scarf, it was beautiful, a strong, tight wool, around his neck. He took everything from me, everything."

Nicole went up to Michael and gently, oh so gently, pressed her finger over his lips. She couldn't stop crying, and she couldn't stop shaking. It was funny how sometimes, your body just did things, without your mind. She knew she had to be strong now, to be a mother and a wife and a lawyer, but her body just shook. Maybe that's what happened with her and Winston. Her body just reacted to a male body's nearness. And maybe that's what happened with Michael and Winston. All his intelligence and his education and his morality, they just weren't with him in that moment on Turnabout night. His body just reacted. He wasn't a murderer, and she wasn't an adulterer. They were just two people who had made terrible mistakes.

Two policemen walked into the living room. "Officer, please arrest Michael Fisher for the murder of Winston Bigelow. You'll need to warn him." She turned to the family, in a huddled clump in front of her. "Thank you for coming to get me, Girls, you did the right thing. You protected your mother." Michael stood up straight, and his daughters let him go.

He turned to Nicole. "I wouldn't have hurt you, I could never do that," he said.

"I know, Dear," she said. She reached up and touched his cheek.

Chapter Eighteen

Meredith walked into her house and slammed the door shut. She had rushed out so quickly with the twins that she hadn't even thrown on a coat, but she felt surprisingly warm. It must be the heat of the moment. She had just faced a murderer, and he was her neighbor. Michael Fisher was a lawyer, a husband, a father. Meredith had waved to him and chatted with his wife, and his daughters had babysat for her children. And two days ago, he had killed a man. Now Michael was at the Wilmette police station. Meredith had stayed with Nicole while she called a lawyer for her husband and a friend for herself.

Meredith didn't know how the community would respond to the Fishers. When a mother had cancer, neighbor women brought meals and drove to appointments and babysat. But what did they do when, prompted by her adultery, a Wilmette woman's husband murdered another Wilmette woman's husband? Certainly there would be gossip. Would Sally down the block bring turkey tetrazzini? Would Tom across the street snow blow their sidewalk? Meredith didn't know.

"Mom, what's going on?" A large spoon in her hand, Maggie popped her head through the kitchen doorway.

"What are you doing?" Meredith asked. A large pot of water bubbled on the stove, as did a small pan of sauce, which spurted red dots onto the stove top and Maggie's Wilmette Wolves tee shirt. If Maggie were wearing her gym suit as clothes, Meredith had definitely lost track of her laundry responsibilities.

"We're making dinner," Lucy announced, looking up from carefully chopping carrots. "It's pasta and salad. You're going to love it."

"I already love it." Meredith touched Lucy's back. She wasn't sure if the girls were cooking to help her, or simply out of desperation, but they were showing a can-do spirit, and possibly actual consideration for her.

"Is everything okay at the Fishers? I saw police cars," Maggie asked nonchalantly.

Meredith paused. Trying to hide the situation would probably do more harm than good. Seventh grade girls seemed to know everything that might have any tangential bearing on the life of someone they knew, and, although Ricky Bigelow was in ninth grade, he undoubtedly was on the same soccer team as the brother of a girl in her science class. And of course, as their neighborhood babysittee, Maggie was the go-to girl for the story on Kelsey and Abby Fisher. This was Meredith's chance to explain the situation in an adult manner.

"Have you heard about Mr. Bigelow?"

"Duh," said Maggie, confirming Meredith's suspicions. "Someone killed him."

"Yes," said Meredith. "The situation is very complicated, but I'm afraid that Mr. Fisher may have been involved."

"Abby's Dad killed somebody?" Lucy asked, her chopping knife suspended in mid-air.

"It's very complicated, but that's what it looks like. Abby and Kelsey are fine," yeah, right, Meredith thought, that'll be the day, "and Mr. Fisher is in jail. So you have nothing to worry about." That was enough for now.

The doorbell rang. "Mom, dinner's almost ready." Maggie sounded annoyed.

"I'm sorry, Honey. It smells really good. Hopefully this won't take long. If it does, start without me, I know you're hungry." She hurried to the front door. The police should be able to handle the Fisher situation tonight, but maybe they had a few quick questions.

Meredith opened the door. Shawna was standing on the steps. Meredith didn't know they made winter jackets that tight across the chest. Her leather boots had tassels on the side which jiggled as she stomped the snow off her feet. "I'm sorry to bother you, but I really want to talk to you. Can I come in?"

Reluctantly, Meredith admitted Shawna to her home. Shawna had dropped the girls off, but, in the six months that they had lived here, she had never been inside the house before.

"Your house is beautiful," Shawna said politely.

"Thanks," nodded Meredith. She gestured toward the couch. "We're just about to eat dinner, but you can sit down for a minute. What's up?"

Shawna sat, and her skirt tugged up. Perching on the edge of an old upholstered chair, Meredith pulled out the waistband of her slacks to ease them over her belly. She tried to look dignified, but she was afraid she just looked old.

"It's about Alex. I'm afraid – he's always at the hospital, he says he is, but it's a lot."

"I think you need to talk to Alex about that, not me." Meredith knew that awful feeling. It wasn't just that Alex was gone a lot, but also that, even when he was home, he wasn't entirely present. Meredith had thought at first that it was because they had been married a while, that it was just a phase, or maybe an inevitable transition from romance into companionship. But, no, the problem was right in front of her. And it needed to button its blouse.

"But I'm afraid – he's with you." Shawna blushed. "I know it's hard to believe," she said, gesturing vaguely between them, "but I think he might be interested in you."

"Yes," Meredith said, and Shawna looked startled. "It is hard to believe. It was hard for me to believe it when he …." Meredith gestured vaguely toward Shawna. She was not going to spill her guts to this woman. Shawna did not deserve it. "This has nothing to do with me. You need to talk to your husband."

"But you're wrong about that. It does have to do with you. I was wrong, I know that now. I was a kid, I was 24 years old." Meredith winced. "I was single, I wanted a boyfriend or a husband, there was nothing wrong with that. I met Alex. He was handsome, he was a doctor, and he liked me. I couldn't believe it. And yes, he was married, but that didn't matter. It was his marriage, not mine, I didn't know you, I thought it was just a mistake. I mean, he was married to somebody old, he didn't want her anymore, that shouldn't stand in the way of real love and happiness. I didn't owe you anything, he did, and if he wanted me instead of you, he had his reasons. It was romantic."

Meredith sat there, white. She had never heard Shawna say so many words in a row. "Why are you telling me this?"

"I'm telling you because I was wrong. I was young and stupid, and I didn't understand. I was twenty-four. I'd never even had a serious boyfriend, let alone a husband."

Meredith looked at Shawna. In a few years Kelsey Fisher would be twenty-four. She would trade her terry cloth shorts with Juicy on the butt for gray sweats with Sigma Tau on it, but she still wouldn't have a clear idea of her personal responsibilities, especially when it came to love. Heck, Meredith didn't always know, and Alex certainly didn't – or he just didn't care, which was a lot worse. "So now you think Alex wants to turn around and dump you for me – and now you know how I felt when you did that to me, and – what?"

Shawna swallowed. "First, I want to say how sorry I am. I should have thought of you, I should have thought of Maggie and Lucy. I did owe you something, as human beings. But I'd seen so many movies…."

"Forget the movies. Keep going."

"And second, I'm sorry because I knew that Alex liked me, and I – well, I flirted, I guess, I tried to get him. I guess I knew that was wrong, in a way, but I liked him. I thought it was his job to say no, and if he didn't, well…."

Meredith wasn't sure this was a second point, as regards Shawna and her behavior. As for Alex and his conduct, it was a very good point indeed. All these years, Meredith had blamed Alex for being a cheating husband who left her. But at bottom, she had felt that it would be very hard for a man to resist Shawna and stay loyal to her, with her extra ten pounds and character lines and the demands of family life. But she had blamed Shawna, the faceless, irresistible siren, who now had a face and cowboy boots and large diamond rings. When the real question was, not how evil was Shawna, but what in the hell was Alex doing now? Had he come to realize he made a terrible mistake in marrying Shawna, that he really loved Meredith – or did he just want what he didn't have, and was he going to turn around and do it to her again?

"The thing is," Shawna continued, and she started to tear up, "I love Alex, and we're married now, and I want to stay married. And I know that was you once, and I know now what I did, and maybe I don't have any right, but I'm asking you, please – don't do to me what I did to you. I don't know why he is turning to you now. But please, don't take Alex away from me."

"I don't want revenge on you, Shawna," Meredith said, and surprisingly, she meant it. "And Alex – he has been spending more time here, but we are not – having an affair." Not exactly, she thought. Not yet. "I don't know what Alex wants," she said weakly.

"I know what I want," said Shawna. "What do you want?"

"Shawna!" Lucy ran into the living room and threw her arms around her neck. While Meredith found this extravagant display a little annoying, she was happy to see a red, saucy smear on the collar of Shawna's silk blouse. "Are we going to your house?"

"No, Luce, I came to talk to your mom. Can you give us a minute?" Shawna removed Lucy's moist hands and tapped her nose.

"Sure. I'm going to watch TV. You'll like the dinner, Mom. It's delicious." Lucy made disturbing licking and slurping noises and then bolted from the room.

"Hi, Shawna. Mom, I'm going to do my homework. I left you a plate." Glancing suspiciously over her shoulder, Maggie began to climb the stairs.

"Thanks, Honey. That was really sweet of you." Meredith looked at Shawna. "I think you should go now."

Shawna looked surprised. "Okay," she said, standing up. "You'll think about what I said?"

"Be careful driving home. It looks like the snow is picking up," Meredith said, as she opened the front door.

Shawna jingled her way down the front steps, and Meredith shut the door. She walked back to the kitchen. The empty Ragu jar and spaghetti box sat on the counter next to the dirty dishes. No miracles had occurred, but on the kitchen table, on top of a plastic placemat displaying the periodic table of the elements, rested a large plate of pasta with marinara sauce and parmesan cheese. Next to it were a small salad in a cereal bowl, and a glass of red wine, filled to the brim. She could hear the voice of Marge Simpson from the TV in the next room, and the sound of pacing above her, which meant that Maggie was memorizing her French vocabulary words. Across the street, a family had shattered, but tonight, after all her suffering, and all her hard work, this family, the three of them, was intact. Meredith took a sip of wine and a bite of spaghetti. It did taste delicious.

Acknowledgements

With special thanks to Emily, Eliza, Julia, Rebecca, Leslie, Laurel, and Colleen, who asked for another book; to Jeff, my first reader, for his support and helpful suggestions; to Carl, Shane, David, Caroline, Jerome, and my mother, Margo Reisman, for their interest and encouragement; to Adam Sheffield, for taking the cover photograph; and to my father, psychologist and mystery writer John Reisman, whose novel *The Mad Bunny* inspired the last line.

About the Author

Hope Sheffield grew up in Rochester, New York, and then moved to Memphis, Tennessee, where she graduated from high school. She earned a degree in psychology at Harvard College. Although she greatly enjoyed Harvard Law School, her legal career was brief. She and her husband have four adult daughters and a teenage son. The author now lives with her husband and son on Chicago's North Shore. *Turnabout* is her third Meredith Bennett mystery, following *Blood Mother* and *The Inflatable Man*.